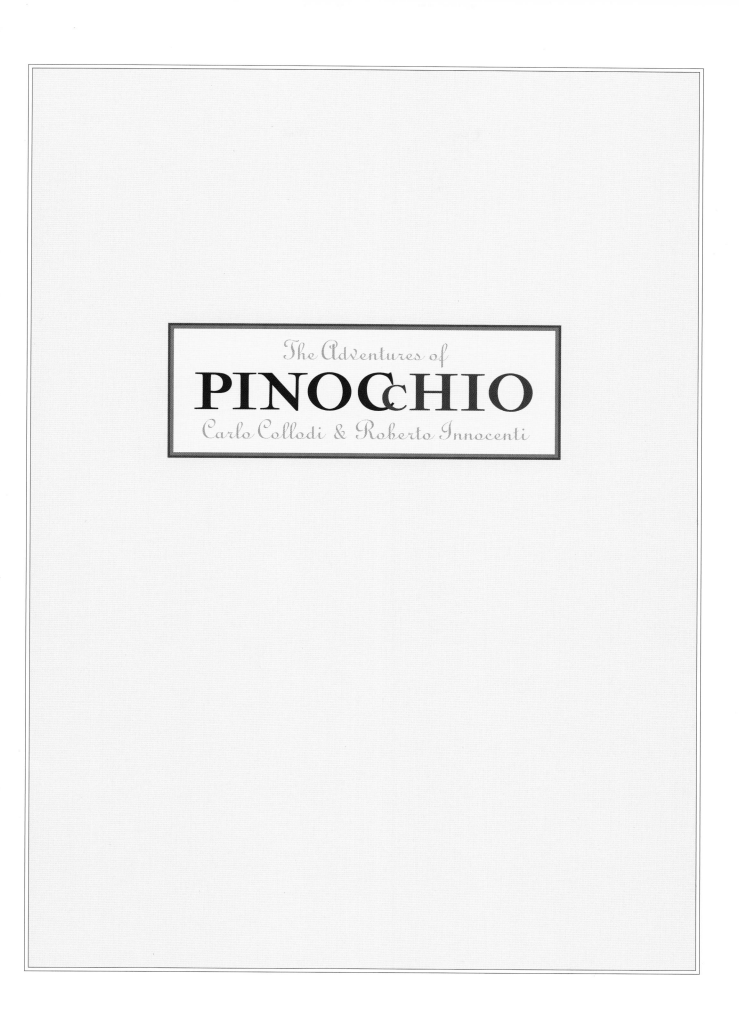

The Adventures of

PINOCCHIO

Carlo Collodi & Roberto Innocenti

Creative Editions

PRESENTS

The Adventures of

PINOCCHIO

Carlo Collodi & Roberto Innocenti

DESIGNED BY RITA MARSHALL

Illustrations copyright © 1988 and 2005 Roberto Innocenti

Published in 2005 by Creative Editions

123 South Broad Street, Mankato, MN 56001 USA

Creative Editions is an imprint of The Creative Company.

Designed by Rita Marshall

Printed in China

Library of Congress Cataloging-in-Publication Data

Collodi, Carlo, 1826-1890.

[Avventure di Pinocchio. English]

The adventures of Pinocchio / by Carlo Collodi;

illustrated by Roberto Innocenti; translated by M.A. Murray.

Summary: A wooden puppet full of tricks and mischief,

with a talent for getting into and out of trouble, wants

more than anything else to become a real boy.

ISBN 978-1-56846-190-8

[1. Fairy tales. 2. Puppets—Fiction.]

I. Innocenti, Roberto, ill.

II. Murray, M.A. (Mary Alice).

III. Title.

PZ8.C7Pi 2004

[Fic]—dc22   2003062740

4 5 3

To Carlo Collodi and
my daughter Alessandra

Other books by Roberto Innocenti

Cinderella

Written by Charles Perrault

Rose Blanche

Written by Christophe Gallaz

Christmas Carol

Written by Charles Dickens

Nutcracker

Written by E. T. A. Hoffmann

The Last Resort

Written by J. Patrick Lewis

Erika's Story

Written by Ruth Vander Zee

The Adventures of PINOCCHIO

Carlo Collodi & Roberto Innocenti

{ Chapter 1 }

Master Cherry finds a strange piece of wood

nce upon a time there was—

"A king!" my little readers will instantly exclaim.

No, children, you are wrong. Once upon a time there was a piece of wood.

This wood was not valuable; it was only a common log like those that are burned in stoves and fireplaces in winter to make a cheerful blaze and warm the room.

I cannot say how it came to be, but one fine day this piece of wood was lying in the shop of an old carpenter by the name of Master Antonio. Everybody called him Master Cherry, however, on account of the end of his nose, which was always as red and polished as a ripe cherry.

No sooner had Master Cherry set eyes on this piece of wood than his face beamed with delight. Rubbing his hands together with satisfaction, he said softly, "This wood has come at just the right moment. It will make the perfect leg for a little table."

Having said this, he picked up a sharp ax to remove the bark and the rough surface. But just as he was about to deliver the first blow, he heard a very small voice say, "Don't strike me hard!"

Imagine the astonishment of good old Master Cherry!

He turned his terrified eyes all around the room to discover from where the little voice could possibly have come, but he saw nobody! He looked under the bench—

nobody; he looked into a cupboard that was always shut—nobody; he looked into a basket of shavings and sawdust—nobody; he even opened the door of the shop and glanced into the street—and still nobody. Who, then, could it be?

"I see how it is," he said, laughing and scratching his wig. "Evidently that little voice was just my imagination. Now let's start again."

He picked up the ax once again and delivered a tremendous blow to the piece of wood.

"Oh! Oh! You hurt me!" cried the same little voice.

This time Master Cherry was petrified. His eyes and mouth widened with fright, and his tongue hung out almost to the end of his chin. As soon as he had recovered the use of his speech, he began to say, stuttering and trembling with fear, "But where on Earth can that little voice have come from that said 'Oh! Oh!'? There's certainly not a living soul here. Is it possible that this piece of wood could have learned to cry and lament like a child? I can't believe it. This piece of wood is a log for fuel like all the others, and thrown on the fire it would only suffice to boil a saucepan of beans. How then? Can anyone be hidden inside it? If anyone is inside, so much the worse for him. I'll show him!"

This said, Master Cherry seized the poor piece of wood and started beating it against the walls of the room without mercy.

Then he stopped to listen for the little voice. He waited two minutes—nothing; five minutes—nothing; ten minutes—still nothing.

"I see how it is," he said again, forcing himself to laugh and pushing up his wig. "Evidently the little voice that said 'Oh! Oh!' was just my imagination! Let's start again."

But by this time, Master Cherry was quite frightened, so he tried to sing to give himself a little courage.

Putting the ax aside, he picked up his plane to smooth and polish the wood. But while he was running it up and down, he heard the same little voice say, laughing, "Stop it! You're tickling me!"

This time poor Master Cherry fell down as if he had been struck by lightning. When at last he opened his eyes, he found himself lying on the floor.

His face was quite changed. Even the end of his nose, instead of being crimson, as it nearly always was, had become blue from fright.

{ Chapter 2 }

Geppetto makes a wonderful puppet

t that moment, someone knocked on the door.

"Come in," said the carpenter, not having the strength to rise to his feet.

A lively little old man immediately walked into the shop. His name was Geppetto. When the boys of the neighborhood wanted to tease him, however, they called him "Polendina," because his yellow wig resembled a pudding made of Indian corn. But woe to anyone who called Geppetto Polendina, as he became furious whenever he heard it.

"Good day, Master Antonio," said Geppetto. "What are you doing there on the floor?"

"I am teaching the ants to read."

"May it do you good!"

"What has brought you here, neighbor Geppetto?"

"My legs. But Master Antonio, I have come to ask a favor of you."

"At your service," replied the carpenter, rising to his knees.

"This morning an idea came into my head."

"Let's hear it."

"I thought I would make a beautiful wooden puppet—a wonderful puppet that would know how to dance, do tricks, and leap like an acrobat. With this puppet I would travel

around the world to earn a piece of bread and a glass of wine. What do you think?"

"Bravo, Polendina!" exclaimed the same little voice. Again, it was impossible to say from where it came.

Hearing himself called Polendina, Geppetto became as red as the comb of a rooster from rage, and turning to the carpenter, he said in a fury, "Why did you insult me?"

"Who insulted you?"

"You called me Polendina!"

"I did not."

"Are you saying I called myself Polendina? It was you, I say!"

"No!"

"Yes!"

"No!"

"Yes!"

As they became more and more angry, their words turned to blows, and they flew at each other, biting and scratching.

When the fight was over, Master Antonio held Geppetto's yellow wig, and Geppetto discovered that the gray wig belonging to the carpenter was clenched between his teeth.

"Give me back my wig," shouted Master Antonio.

"And you return mine, and then let us apologize."

The two old men, having each recovered his own wig, shook hands and swore that they would remain friends to the end of their lives.

"Well, then, Geppetto," said the carpenter, to prove that there were no hard feelings, "what is the favor you wish of me?"

"I want a little wood to make my puppet. Will you give me some?"

Master Antonio was delighted, and he immediately went to the bench and fetched the piece of wood that had frightened him so. Just as he was about to give it to his friend, however, the piece of wood gave a shake and, wriggling violently out of his hands, struck as hard as it could against the shins of poor Geppetto.

"Ah! Is that the courteous way you give gifts, Master Antonio? You almost crippled me!"

"I swear to you that it wasn't I!"

"Are you suggesting that I hit myself?"

"The wood is entirely to blame!"

"I know that it was the wood, but it was you that hit my legs with it!"

"I did not hit you!"

"Liar!"

"Geppetto, don't insult me, or I'll call you Polendina!"

"Donkey!"

"Polendina!"

"Monkey!"

"Polendina!"

"Baboon!"

"Polendina!"

Upon hearing himself called Polendina for the third time, Geppetto, blind with rage, flew at the carpenter, and they fought once more.

When the battle was over, Master Antonio had two more scratches on his nose, and Geppetto had lost two buttons on his jacket. Their accounts being settled, they shook hands and swore to remain good friends for the rest of their lives.

Geppetto thanked Master Antonio and, carrying off his fine piece of wood, limped back home.

{ Chapter 3 }

The puppet is named Pinocchio

eppetto lived in a small, ground-floor room under a staircase. His furniture could not have been simpler—a rickety chair, a poor bed, and a broken-down table. At the end of the room there appeared to be a fireplace with a roaring fire, but the fire was nothing more than a painting. By the fire was a painted saucepan that boiled cheerfully, sending out a cloud of steam that looked exactly like real steam.

After he returned home, Geppetto took out his tools and began to carve his puppet.

"What name shall I give him?" he said to himself. "I think I'll call him Pinocchio. It's a name that will bring him luck. I once knew a whole family called Pinocchio. There was Pinocchio the father, Pinocchia the mother, and Pinocchi the children, and all of them did quite well. The richest of them was a beggar."

Having found a name for his puppet, Geppetto began to work in earnest. Soon he had carved the puppet's hair, forehead, and eyes.

Imagine his astonishment when he noticed that the eyes he had just finished moved—and looked directly at him!

Geppetto bristled and said in an angry voice, "Wicked wooden eyes, why do you look at me?"

No one answered.

He then began to carve the nose, but no sooner had he finished it than it began to

grow. And it grew, and grew, and grew until it had become an immense nose that seemed as if it would never end.

Poor Geppetto tried to cut it short, but the more he cut, the longer that impertinent nose became!

The mouth was not even completed when it began to laugh and mock him.

"Stop laughing!" Geppetto scolded, but he might as well have spoken to the wall. "Stop laughing, I say!"

The mouth then ceased laughing, but stuck out its tongue as far as it would go.

Geppetto pretended not to see this and continued his work. After the mouth was finished, he fashioned the chin, the throat, the shoulders, the stomach, the arms, and the hands.

The hands were barely finished when Geppetto felt his wig snatched from his head. He turned around, and what did he see? He saw his yellow wig in the puppet's hand.

"Pinocchio! Give me back my wig!"

But instead of returning it, Pinocchio put it on his own head, nearly smothering himself.

This insolent behavior saddened Geppetto more than anything ever had. "You young rascal!" he said. "You are not yet completed, and you are already showing a lack of respect for your father! That is bad, my boy, very bad!"

And he dried a tear.

The legs and the feet remained to be done.

When Geppetto finished the feet, he received a kick on the point of his nose.

"I deserve it!" he said to himself. "I should have thought of it sooner! Now it's too late!"

He then took the puppet by the arms and placed him on the floor to teach him to walk.

At first, Pinocchio's legs were stiff, and he could not move, but Geppetto led him by the hand and showed him how to put one foot in front of the other.

Once his legs became flexible, Pinocchio began to walk by himself and to run about the room. Then, noticing the front door was open, he jumped out the door and escaped down the street.

Poor Geppetto rushed after him but was not able to catch him, for that rascal Pinocchio leaped in front of him like a hare, and knocking his wooden feet against the pavement made as much clatter as twenty pairs of clogs.

"Stop him! Stop him!" shouted Geppetto. But the people in the street, seeing a wooden puppet running like a racehorse, stood still in astonishment, and laughed, and laughed, and laughed.

At last, as good luck would have it, a policeman arrived who, hearing the uproar, thought that a colt had escaped from his master. Planting himself courageously in the middle of the road with his legs apart, he waited with the determined purpose of stopping him, and thus preventing the chance of worse disasters.

When Pinocchio, still at some distance, saw the policeman barricading the street, he tried to take him by surprise and pass between his legs.

The policeman, without budging, snatched him cleverly by the nose—it was an immense nose of ridiculous proportions that seemed especially made for policemen to grab—and returned him to Geppetto. Geppetto intended to pull Pinocchio's ears at once to punish him. But imagine his surprise when he could not find them! And do you know the reason? It was that, in his hurry to carve the puppet, he had forgotten to make them.

So instead, Geppetto took him by the collar, and as he was leading him away, he said, shaking his head threateningly, "Just wait 'til we get home! I'll teach you such a lesson—"

When Pinocchio heard this, he threw himself on the ground and would not take another step. At once a crowd of spectators and curious people circled around them.

"Poor puppet!" said several. "He's right not to want to return home! Who knows how Geppetto, that bad old man, will beat him!"

And others added, "Geppetto seems a good man. But with boys he's a regular tyrant! If that poor puppet is left in his hands, he is quite capable of tearing him to pieces!"

Indeed, they all said so much that the policeman at last set Pinocchio free and hauled Geppetto off to prison. The poor man, unable to find the words to defend himself, bawled like a calf, and as he was being led away, he wailed, "Wretched boy! And to think that I worked so hard to make him a well-behaved puppet! But it serves me right! I should have thought of it sooner!"

What happened afterwards is a story that really is beyond belief, but I shall nevertheless tell it to you in the following chapters.

{ Chapter 4 }

Pinocchio meets the talking cricket

❦

ow, children, I must tell you that while poor Geppetto was being taken to prison, through no fault of his own, that imp Pinocchio, finding himself free from the clutches of the policeman, ran off as fast as his legs could carry him. In his hurry to get home, he rushed across the fields and jumped high banks, thorn hedges, and ditches full of water, exactly as a rabbit would have done if pursued by hunters.

When he reached home, he found the front door ajar. He pushed it open, went in, and, after securing the latch behind him, sat down on the floor with a great sigh of relief.

But his satisfaction did not last long, for he heard someone in the room saying, "Cri-cri-cri!"

"Who calls me?" said Pinocchio in a fright.

"It is I!"

Pinocchio turned around and saw a big cricket crawling slowly up the wall.

"Tell me, cricket, who are you?"

"I am the talking cricket, and I have lived in this room for more than one hundred years."

"Well, now this room is mine," said the puppet. "So do me a favor and go away at once, and don't look back."

"I won't go," answered the cricket, "until I have told you a great truth."

"Tell it to me then—and be quick about it."

"Woe to those children who rebel against their parents and run away from home. They will never come to any good in this world, and sooner or later, they will repent bitterly."

"Sing away, cricket, as you please, and for as long as you will. I have already made up my mind to run away tomorrow at daybreak, because if I stay here, I'll suffer the same fate as all other boys. I'll be sent to school. And to tell you the truth, I have no desire to learn. It's much more fun to run after butterflies, or to climb trees and take young birds out of their nests."

"Poor little fool! Don't you know that if all you do is play, you'll grow up to be a perfect donkey, and that everyone will make fun of you?"

"Hold your tongue, you wicked croaker!" shouted Pinocchio.

But the cricket, who was patient and wise, instead of becoming angry at Pinocchio's bad behavior, continued in the same tone. "If you don't want to go to school, then why not learn a trade, if only to enable you to earn an honest living!"

"I'll tell you why," replied Pinocchio, who was beginning to lose his patience. "Among all the trades in the world, there is only one that really tickles my fancy."

"And what is that?"

"To eat, drink, sleep, and amuse myself, and to lead a vagabond life from morning to night."

"As a rule," said the talking cricket with the same composure, "all those who follow that trade almost always end up either in the hospital or in prison."

"Be careful, you wicked croaker! Woe to you if I become angry!"

"Poor Pinocchio. I really pity you!"

"Why?"

"Because you are a puppet, and—what is worse—you have a wooden head."

At these words Pinocchio jumped up in a rage, snatched a mallet from the bench, and threw it at the talking cricket.

Perhaps he never meant to hit him, but unfortunately the mallet struck the cricket right on the head. The poor creature scarcely had time to cry "Cri-cri-cri," and there he was, flattened against the wall.

❧

{ Chapter 5 }

Pinocchio makes a funny omelet

ight soon fell, and Pinocchio, remembering that he had not eaten all day, began to feel a gnawing in his stomach that very much resembled an appetite.

But boys' appetites grow quickly, and after a few minutes, his appetite became a terrible hunger, and in no time his hunger became a ravenous beast.

Poor Pinocchio ran to the fireplace to devour the contents of the boiling saucepan he saw there, but the saucepan was only painted on the wall. Imagine his surprise! His nose, which was already long, grew at least three inches longer.

Then he began to run around the room, searching in drawers and every imaginable place, in hopes of finding a bit of dry bread, a crust, a bone left by a dog, a little moldy pudding, a fish bone, a cherry pit—anything on which to gnaw. But he found absolutely nothing.

Meanwhile, his hunger grew and grew. Poor Pinocchio had no other relief than yawning, and his yawns were so tremendous that sometimes his mouth almost reached to where his ears ought to have been. After he yawned, he was even hungrier and felt as if he were going to faint.

Then he began to cry desperately and said, "The talking cricket was right. I was wrong to rebel against my father and to run away from home. If my father were here now, I would not be dying of hunger! Oh! What a dreadful illness hunger is!"

Just then, he thought he saw something in a pile of wood shavings—something round and white that looked like a hen's egg. He leaped to his feet and grabbed it. It was indeed an egg!

Pinocchio's joy was indescribable. Fearing it was all part of a dream, he kept turning the egg over and over in his hands, feeling it and kissing it. "And now, how will I cook it?" he wondered. "Should I make an omelet? Would it be tastier to poach? Or should I simply boil it? No, the quickest way of all is to fry it. I am in such a hurry to eat!"

He quickly built a small fire and placed the pan over it. Instead of oil or butter, he poured a little water into the pan, and when the water began to steam, *crack!* He broke the shell over it so that the contents would drop in. But instead of the egg white and the yolk, out popped a very friendly little chicken, who bowed and said, "A thousand thanks, Master

Pinocchio, for saving me the trouble of breaking the shell. Take care, and give my best to your family!"

And with that, the chicken spread its wings, darted through the open window, and flew away.

The poor puppet stood there as if bewitched, with his eyes fixed, his mouth open, and the empty shell still in his hand. As he recovered from his stupor, however, he began to howl and stomp his feet in desperation.

"Oh! The talking cricket was right. If I had not run away from home, and if my father were here now, I would not be dying of hunger! Oh! What a dreadful illness hunger is!"

And as his stomach cried out more than ever, and he did not know how to quiet it, he decided he would leave the house and walk through the neighborhood in hopes of finding some charitable person who would give him a piece of bread.

{ Chapter 6 }

Pinocchio's feet are burned off

t was a wild and stormy night. Thunder crashed, and the lightning was so violent that the sky seemed to be on fire. A blustery wind whistled angrily and swept rising clouds of dust across the countryside, causing trees to creak and groan.

Pinocchio had a great fear of thunder, but his hunger was stronger than his fear. He closed the front door behind him and ran to the village, which he soon reached, panting, with his tongue hanging out like a dog's.

But he found the town dark and deserted. The shops were closed, the windows shut, and there was not so much as a dog in the street. It seemed like the land of the dead.

Pinocchio, driven by desperation and hunger, rang the bell of the first house he came to, saying to himself, "That will bring somebody."

And so it did. A little old man appeared at a window with a nightcap on his head, and called to him angrily, "What do you want at such an hour?"

"Would you be kind enough to give me some bread?"

"Wait there. I'll be right back," said the little old man, thinking he was dealing with one of those rascally boys who amuse themselves at night by ringing the doorbells of respectable people to rouse them from their beds.

After a half-minute, the voice of the same little old man shouted to Pinocchio, "Come underneath the window and hold out your cap."

Pinocchio pulled off his cap; but just as he held it out, an enormous basin of water was poured down on him, drenching him from head to foot as if he was a pot of dried-up geraniums.

He returned home like a wet chicken, quite exhausted with fatigue and hunger. No longer having the strength to stand, he sat down and rested his damp and muddy feet on the stove full of burning embers.

Then he fell asleep. And while he slept, his feet, which were wooden, caught fire, and little by little they burned away.

Pinocchio continued to sleep and snore as if his feet belonged to someone else. At last, around daybreak, he was awakened by a knocking at the door.

"Who's there?" he asked, yawning and rubbing his eyes.

"It is I!" answered a voice.

It was the voice of Geppetto.

{ Chapter 7 }

Geppetto gives the puppet something to eat

oor Pinocchio, whose eyes were still half closed, had not yet discovered that his feet had been burned off. When he heard his father's voice, he slipped off his stool to run and open the door. But instead, he stumbled and fell flat on the floor, making as much noise as if a sack of wooden spoons had been thrown from a fifth-story window.

"Open the door!" shouted Geppetto from the street.

"Dear Father, I can't," answered the puppet, crying and rolling about on the ground.

"Why not?"

"Because my feet have been eaten."

"And who has eaten your feet?"

"The cat," said Pinocchio, seeing the cat, who was amusing herself by making some wood shavings dance with her forepaws.

"Open the door, I tell you!" demanded Geppetto. "If you don't, when I get into the house you will have the cat-o'-nine-tails from me!"

"I can't stand up, believe me. Oh, poor me! Poor me! I'll have to walk on my knees for the rest of my life!"

Geppetto, believing that all this lamentation was just another one of the puppet's tricks, climbed up the wall and entered his house through a window.

He was very angry, and at first he did nothing but scold. But when he saw Pinocchio lying on the ground without feet, he was overcome with pity. He took him in his arms, kissed him, and said a thousand endearing things to him. And as the tears ran down his cheeks, he cried, "My dear little Pinocchio! How did you manage to burn your feet?"

"I don't know, Father, but believe me, it has been a horrible night—one that I'll never forget. It thundered and lightninged, and I was very hungry. And then the talking cricket said to me, 'It serves you right! You have been wicked and you deserve it.' And I said to him, 'Be careful, cricket!' And he said, 'You are a puppet, and you have a wooden head,' and then I threw a mallet at him, and he died, but it was his own fault, for I didn't want to kill him, and the proof of it is that I put the frying pan on the stove, but a chicken flew out and said, 'Give my best to your family!' And then I got even hungrier, and a little old man in a nightcap said to me, 'Come underneath the window and hold out your cap,' then he poured a basinful of water on my head. I returned home, and because I was still very hungry, I put my feet on the stove to dry them, and then you returned. Now I find my feet burned off, and I am still hungry, but I no longer have any feet! Oh, oh, oh!" And poor Pinocchio began to cry so loudly that he could be heard a mile away.

Geppetto, who from this jumbled account had understood only one thing—that the puppet was dying of hunger—drew from his pocket three pears, gave them to Pinocchio, and said, "I had intended to eat these three pears for breakfast, but I will give them to you instead. I hope they will do you good."

"If you want me to eat them, be kind enough to peel them for me."

"Peel them?" said Geppetto, astonished. "I should never have thought, my boy, that you were so fussy. That is bad! In this world, you must learn to eat everything, for there is no telling what you may be given."

"You may be right," interrupted Pinocchio, "but I won't eat fruit that has not been peeled. I can't stand the skin."

So, Geppetto fetched a knife and, arming himself with patience, peeled the three pears and put the peelings on a corner of the table.

After eating the first pear in two mouthfuls, Pinocchio was about to throw away the core, but Geppetto caught hold of his arm. "Don't throw that away," said Geppetto. "In this world, everything may be of use."

"But I certainly won't eat the core!" shouted the puppet, turning on him like a viper.

"Very well," Geppetto replied, without losing his temper.

And so the three cores, instead of being thrown out of the window, were placed on a corner of the table together with the peelings.

Having eaten, or rather having devoured, the three pears, Pinocchio yawned and said in a fretful tone, "I am as hungry as ever!"

"But, my boy, I have nothing more to give you!"

"Nothing?"

"I have only the peelings and the cores of the three pears."

"Well, then!" said Pinocchio. "If there is nothing else, I'll eat some peelings."

And he began to eat them. At first he made a wry face, but then he quickly swallowed the pear skins one after the other. Then he ate the cores. And when he had eaten everything in sight, he put his hands on his hips and said joyfully, "Ah! Now I feel comfortable."

"You see?" said Geppetto. "I was right when I said that everything may be of use in this world. We can never know, my dear boy, what may happen to us!"

{ Chapter 8 }

Geppetto sells his coat to buy a spelling book

s soon as Pinocchio had satisfied his hunger, he began to cry and grumble because he wanted a pair of new feet.

To punish Pinocchio for his naughtiness, Geppetto allowed him to cry and despair for half the day. He then said to him, "Why should I make you new feet? To enable you to run away from home again?"

"I promise," said the puppet, sobbing, "that from now on, I will be good."

"All children," replied Geppetto, "when they want something, say the same thing."

"I promise to go to school and to study so that you will be proud of me."

"All children, when they want something, repeat the same story."

"But I'm not like other children! I'm better than all of them, and I always speak the truth. I promise you, Father, that I will learn a trade, and that I'll be of help to you in your old age."

Although he put on a serious face, Geppetto's eyes were full of tears, and his heart was big with sorrow at seeing poor Pinocchio in such a state. He did not say another word, but taking his tools and two small pieces of well-seasoned wood, he set to work.

In less than an hour, the feet were finished—two little feet so beautiful they might have been carved by a great sculptor.

Geppetto then said to the puppet, "Shut your eyes and go to sleep!"

Pinocchio shut his eyes and pretended to be asleep.

And while the puppet pretended to sleep, Geppetto, with a little glue that he had melted in an eggshell, fastened the feet in place. He did such a fine job that not even a trace could be seen of where the feet were joined.

As soon as the puppet discovered that he had feet again, he jumped down from the table on which he was lying and began to leap around the room as if he had gone mad with delight.

"To reward you for what you have done for me," said Pinocchio to his father, "I will go to school at once."

"Good boy."

"But to go to school, I'll need some clothes."

Geppetto, who was poor and did not have so much as a cent in his pocket, made the puppet a little suit of flowered paper, a pair of shoes from the bark of a tree, and a cap of bread dough.

Pinocchio ran to look at his reflection in a pot of water, and he was so pleased with his appearance that he said, strutting around like a peacock, "I look like a gentleman!"

"Yes, indeed," answered Geppetto. "It is not fine clothes but clean clothes that make the gentleman."

"By the way," added the puppet, "I can't go to school without a spelling book."

"You're right. But what will we do to get one?"

"That's easy. We'll go to the bookseller and buy it."

"And the money?"

"I have none."

"Neither do I," added the good old man sadly.

Pinocchio, although he was a very merry boy, became sad too, because poverty, when it is real poverty, is understood by everyone—even by children.

"Just a moment!" exclaimed Geppetto, suddenly rising to his feet. Putting on his old, patched coat, he ran out of the house.

He returned shortly, holding in his hand a spelling book for Pinocchio, but the old

coat was gone. The poor man was in his shirt sleeves, even though it was snowing outside.

"Where's your coat, Father?"

"I sold it."

"Why?"

"Because it made me too warm."

Pinocchio understood this answer in an instant, and unable to restrain the impulse of his good heart, sprang up, threw his arms around Geppetto's neck, and kissed him again and again.

{ Chapter 9 }

Pinocchio sells his spelling book to see a show

s soon as it stopped snowing, Pinocchio set out for school with his spelling book under his arm. On the way, he began to imagine a thousand things in his little head, and to build a thousand castles in the air, one more beautiful than the other.

Talking to himself, he said, "Today at school I'll learn to read. Then tomorrow I'll begin to write, and the day after tomorrow to do sums and figures. Then with my skills I'll earn a great deal of money, and with the first coins I have in my pocket, I'll immediately buy a beautiful cloth coat for my father. But what am I saying? Cloth, indeed! It will be made of gold and silver, and it will have diamond buttons. That poor man really deserves it; to buy me books and send me to school, he has remained in his shirt sleeves. And in this cold! Only fathers are capable of such sacrifices."

At that moment, Pinocchio thought he heard music in the distance. It sounded like fifes and the beating of a big drum: *fi-fi-fi, fi-fi-fi, zum, zum, zum, zum.*

He stopped and listened. The sounds came from the end of a street that led to an open square on the seashore.

"What can that music be? What a pity that I have to go to school, or else...."

Pinocchio hesitated, trying to decide what to do. Should I go to school? Or should I go and listen to the fifes?

"Today I'll go and hear the fifes," he finally decided, "and tomorrow I'll go to school."

The more he ran, the clearer the sounds of the fifes and the beating of the big drum became: *fi-fi-fi, zum, zum, zum, zum.*

At last he found himself in the middle of a square full of people, who were all crowding around a building made of wood and canvas painted a thousand colors.

"What is that building?" Pinocchio asked a little boy standing nearby.

"Read the sign, and then you'll know."

"I would gladly read it, but it so happens that today I don't know how to read."

"Bravo, blockhead! Then I'll read it for you. The writing on the sign, in those letters red as fire, says, '*Great Puppet Theater.*'"

"When does the play begin?"

"Right now."

"How much does it cost to get in?"

"Five cents."

Pinocchio, who was in a fever of curiosity, lost all control of himself and said to the little boy, "Would you lend me five cents 'til tomorrow?"

"Ordinarily I would gladly lend it to you," said the boy, "but it so happens that today I cannot."

"I'll sell you my jacket for five cents," said Pinocchio.

"Why do you think I would want a jacket of flowered paper? If it rained, and the paper got wet, it would be impossible to get it off my back."

"Will you buy my shoes?"

"They would be of use only to light a fire."

"How much will you give me for my cap?"

"That would be a fine bargain indeed! A cap made of bread dough! Mice would likely eat it right off my head."

Pinocchio was on pins and needles. He was about to make another offer, but he did not have the courage. He hesitated. At last he said, "Will you give me five cents for this new spelling book?"

"I never buy anything like that from other children," replied the boy, who had much more sense than Pinocchio.

"I'll buy the spelling book for five cents," said a street seller, who had been listening to the conversation.

The book was sold there and then. And to think that poor Geppetto, shivering at home from the cold, had sold his coat to buy his son a spelling book!

{ Chapter 10 }

The show puppets welcome Pinocchio

❦

hen Pinocchio walked into the little puppet theater, an incident occurred that almost caused a riot.

I must tell you that the curtain was up, and the play had already begun.

On the stage, two puppets, named Harlequin and Punchinello, were quarreling with each other—as was typical in puppet plays—and threatening every moment to come to blows.

The audience laughed until they cried as they listened to the bickerings of the two puppets, who gestured and abused each other so naturally that they might have been two real people.

All at once, however, Harlequin stopped and turned to the audience. He pointed to someone far down in the pit of the theater and exclaimed in a dramatic tone, "My goodness! Am I dreaming, or am I awake? Surely that is Pinocchio!"

"It is Pinocchio!" cried Punchinello.

"It is indeed!" cried Miss Rose, peeping from behind the curtains.

"It's Pinocchio! It's Pinocchio!" shouted all the puppets in unison, leaping from all directions onto the stage. "It's our brother Pinocchio! Long live Pinocchio!"

"Pinocchio, come up here," cried Harlequin, "and throw yourself into the arms of your wooden brothers!"

At this affectionate invitation, Pinocchio made a leap from the end of the pit into the reserved seats. Another leap landed him on the head of the orchestra leader, and a final jump put him on the stage.

The kisses, the hugs, the friendly pinches, and the demonstrations of warm, brotherly affection that Pinocchio received from the excited crowd of actors and actresses of the puppet company were beyond compare.

The sight was a very moving one, but the audience, finding the play was stopped, became impatient and began to shout, "We want the play! Go on with the play!"

But they wasted their breath. The puppets, instead of continuing the performance, redoubled their noise, put Pinocchio on their shoulders, and carried him in triumph before the footlights.

At that moment, the Showman appeared. He was very big, and so ugly that the sight of him was enough to frighten anyone. His beard was as black as ink, and so long that it reached from his chin to the ground and was trod upon when he walked. His mouth was as big as an oven, and his eyes were like two lanterns of red glass with lights burning inside them. He carried a large whip made of snakes and foxes' tails twisted together, which he cracked constantly.

At his unexpected appearance, there was a profound silence. No one dared to breathe. A fly might have been heard in the stillness. The poor puppets trembled like leaves.

"Why have you come to raise a disturbance in my theater?" the Showman asked Pinocchio in the gruff voice of a goblin suffering from a severe cold.

"Believe me, honored sir, it was not my fault!"

"Enough! We will settle our accounts tonight."

As soon as the play was over, the Showman went into the kitchen, where a fine sheep, prepared for the Showman's supper, was turning slowly on a spit over the fire.

As there was not enough wood to finish roasting and browning it, he called Harlequin and Punchinello and said to them, "Bring that puppet here. You will find him hanging on a nail. It seems to me that he is made of very dry wood, and I'm sure that if he was thrown on the fire, he would make a beautiful blaze for my roast."

At first, Harlequin and Punchinello hesitated, but a glance from their master made them obey. A short time later, they returned to the kitchen carrying poor Pinocchio, who was wriggling like an eel taken out of the water and crying in despair, "Father! Father! Save me! I don't want to die! I don't want to die!"

{ Chapter 11 }

The Showman sneezes and pardons Pinocchio

ire-Eater, for that was the Showman's name, looked like a terrible man, especially because of the black beard that covered his chest and legs like an apron. In truth, however, he did not have a bad heart. When poor Pinocchio was brought before him, struggling and screaming, "I don't want to die! I don't want to die!" he was quite moved and felt sorry for him. He tried to suppress his feelings for the puppet as long as he could, but soon he could stand it no longer, and he sneezed violently. Upon hearing the sneeze, Harlequin, who up to that moment had been in the deepest despair, and bowed down like a weeping willow, became quite cheerful. Leaning towards Pinocchio, he whispered, "Good news, brother! The Showman has sneezed, and that is a sign that he pities you, and that you are saved!"

You must know that while most men weep, or at least pretend to dry their eyes when they feel compassion for somebody, Fire-Eater had the habit of sneezing whenever he was really overcome with emotion.

After he sneezed, the Showman shouted to Pinocchio, "Stop your crying! Your lamentations have given me a pain in my stomach. I feel a spasm that almost—*achoo! Achoo!*"

"Bless you!" said Pinocchio.

"Thank you. And your father and mother, are they still alive?" asked Fire-Eater.

"My father, yes. But I never knew my mother."

"What a sorrow it would be for your poor old father if I were to have you thrown amongst those burning coals! Poor old man! How I pity him! *Achoo! Achoo! Achoo!*"

"Bless you!" said Pinocchio.

"Thank you. All the same, some compassion is due to me. As you see, I have no more wood to finish roasting my mutton, and to tell you the truth, under the circumstances, you would have been of great use! However, I have had pity on you, so I must not complain. Instead, I will burn one of the puppets belonging to my company. Guards!"

Two wooden guards immediately responded to his call. They were very tall and very thin. They wore hats on their heads, and held unsheathed swords in their hands.

The Showman said to them in a hoarse voice, "Take Harlequin, bind him securely, and throw him on the fire to burn. My mutton must be well roasted."

Imagine poor Harlequin! His terror was so great that his legs buckled under him, and he fell face-first onto the ground.

At this agonizing sight, Pinocchio threw himself at the Showman's feet and, bathing his long beard in tears, said in a pleading voice, "Have pity, Sir Fire-Eater!"

"There are no sirs here," the Showman answered severely.

"Have pity, Sir Knight!"

"There are no knights here!"

"Have pity, Commander!"

"There are no commanders here!"

"Have pity, your Excellence!"

Upon hearing himself called "Excellence," the Showman began to smile, becoming at once kinder and more agreeable. He turned to Pinocchio and asked, "Well, what do you want from me?"

"I implore you to pardon poor Harlequin."

"For him there can be no pardon. As I have spared you, he must be put on the fire, for my mutton must be well roasted."

"In that case," cried Pinocchio proudly, rising and throwing down his cap, "in that case, I know my duty. Come, guards! Bind me and throw me amongst the flames. It's not right that poor Harlequin, my true friend, should die for me!"

These words, delivered in a loud, heroic voice, made all the puppets who were present cry. Even the guards wept like babies.

At first, Fire-Eater remained as cold and hard as ice, but little by little he began to melt—and to sneeze. After sneezing four or five times, he opened his arms affectionately and said to Pinocchio, "You are a good, brave boy! Come here and give me a kiss."

Pinocchio ran to him and, climbing like a squirrel up the Showman's beard, deposited a hearty kiss on the point of his nose.

"Then the pardon is granted?" asked poor Harlequin in a faint voice that could hardly be heard.

"The pardon is granted!" answered Fire-Eater. Then he added, sighing and shaking his head, "Very well, then! Tonight I'll have to resign myself to eat my mutton half raw. But next time, woe to him who stands in my way!"

When they learned the news of the pardon, all the puppets ran to the stage, lit the lamps and the chandeliers as if for a full performance, and began to dance merrily. At dawn, they were still dancing.

⚜

{ Chapter 12 }

Fire-Eater becomes generous

he following day, Fire-Eater called Pinocchio aside and asked him, "What is your father's name?"

"Geppetto."

"And what is his trade?"

"That of a very poor man."

"Does he earn much?"

"Earn much? Why, he never has a penny in his pocket. To buy a spelling book for me, he sold the only coat he had to wear—a coat so patched it was not fit to be seen."

"Poor fellow! I feel almost sorry for him! Here are five gold pieces. Go at once and take them to him with my compliments."

Pinocchio thanked the Showman a thousand times. He embraced all of the puppets one by one, even the guards, and then set out for home, filled with joy.

But he had not gone far when he met a fox who was lame in one foot and a cat who was blind in both eyes. They were going along helping each other like good companions in misfortune. The fox, since he was lame, leaned on the cat, and the cat, since he was blind, was guided by the fox.

"Good day, Pinocchio," said the fox, bowing politely.

"How do you know my name?" asked the puppet.

"I know your father well."

"Where did you see him?"

"I saw him yesterday at the door of his house."

"And what was he doing?"

"He was in his shirt sleeves and shivering with cold."

"Poor Father! But after today, he will shiver no more!"

"Why?"

"Because I have become a gentleman."

"A gentleman? You?" said the fox, and he began to laugh rudely and scornfully. The cat began to laugh too, but she combed her whiskers with her forepaws to hide it.

"There's nothing to laugh at," cried Pinocchio angrily. "I don't want to make you envious, but as you can see, I hold five gold pieces."

And he pulled out the money that Fire-Eater had given him.

At the pleasing ring of the money, the fox, with an involuntary movement, stretched out the paw that had just moments ago seemed crippled, and the cat opened wide two eyes that looked like green lanterns. But she shut them again, and so quickly that Pinocchio did not notice.

"And now," asked the fox, "what are you going to do with all that money?"

"First," answered the puppet, "I intend to buy a new coat for my father, made of gold and silver, with diamond buttons, and then I'll buy a spelling book for myself."

"For yourself?"

"Yes indeed, for I intend to go to school and study like a good boy."

"Look at me!" said the fox. "Through my foolish passion for study I have lost a leg."

"Look at me!" said the cat. "Through my foolish passion for study I have lost the sight in both my eyes."

At that moment, a blackbird, perched on a hedge by the road, began his usual song and said, "Pinocchio, don't listen to the advice of bad companions. If you do, you'll be sorry!"

Poor blackbird! If only he had not spoken! The cat, with a great leap, sprang upon him

and, without even giving him time to say "Oh," ate him in a mouthful, feathers and all.

After eating him and cleaning her mouth, the cat shut her eyes again and seemed as blind as ever.

"Poor blackbird!" said Pinocchio to the cat. "Why did you treat him so?"

"I did it to teach him a lesson. Next time he won't meddle in other people's conversations."

They had gone almost halfway to Pinocchio's house when the fox, stopping suddenly, said to the puppet, "Would you like to double your money?"

"In what way?"

"Would you like to turn your five miserable gold pieces into a hundred, a thousand, two thousand?"

"I should think so! But how?"

"It's easy enough. Instead of returning home, you must come with us."

"And where do you want to take me?"

"To the Land of Fools."

Pinocchio reflected a moment, and then said resolutely, "No, I won't go. I'm already close to home, so I'll return to my father, who is waiting for me. Who knows how the poor old man must have suffered yesterday when I didn't come back! I have indeed been a bad son, and the talking cricket was right when he said, 'Disobedient children never come to any good in this world.' To learn that lesson cost me a great deal, for many misfortunes have happened to me. Even yesterday, in Fire-Eater's house, I ran the risk…Oh! It makes me shudder just to think of it!"

"Well, then," said the fox, "you're quite sure you want to go home? Go, then, and so much the worse for you."

"So much the worse for you!" repeated the cat.

"Think well of it, Pinocchio, for you are throwing away a fortune."

"A fortune!" repeated the cat.

"Between today and tomorrow your five gold pieces would have become two thousand."

"Two thousand!" repeated the cat.

"But how is it possible that they could become so many?" asked Pinocchio, his mouth open wide in astonishment.

"I'll explain it to you at once," said the fox. "You must know that in the Land of Fools there is a sacred field called the Field of Miracles. In this field, you dig a little hole, and you put into it, we'll say, one gold piece. You then cover up the hole with a little dirt, water it with two pails of water from the fountain, sprinkle it with two pinches of salt, and then, when night comes, you go quietly to bed. During the night, the gold piece will grow and flower, and in the morning, when you get up and return to the field, what will you find? You'll find a beautiful tree laden with as many gold pieces as a fine ear of corn has kernels in the month of July."

"Suppose," said Pinocchio, more and more bewildered, "that I buried my five gold pieces in that field. How many would I find the following morning?"

"That is an exceedingly easy calculation," replied the fox, "a calculation that you can make on the ends of your fingers. Figure that every gold piece gives you an increase of five hundred. Multiply five hundred by five, and the following morning you would find two thousand five hundred shining gold pieces in your pocket."

"Oh! How delightful!" cried Pinocchio, dancing for joy. "As soon as I've collected those gold pieces, I'll keep two thousand for myself, and make a present of the other five hundred to both of you."

"A present to us?" cried the fox, sounding much offended. "Don't be absurd!"

"Don't be absurd!" repeated the cat.

"We don't work for our own gain," said the fox. "We work only to enrich the lives of others."

"Others!" repeated the cat.

"What good people!" thought Pinocchio. And instantly forgetting his father, the new coat, the spelling book, and all his good resolutions, he said to the fox and the cat, "Let's be off at once! I'll go with you."

{ Chapter 13 }

Pinocchio and his companions stop at the Lobster Inn

 hey walked, and walked, and walked, until at last, towards evening, they arrived dead tired at the Lobster Inn.

"Let's stop here a little while," said the fox, "so that we may have something to eat and rest ourselves for an hour or two. We'll start again at midnight, so we can arrive at the Field of Miracles early tomorrow morning."

They entered the inn and sat down at a table, but none of them had any appetite.

The cat, who was suffering from indigestion and not feeling well at all, could eat only thirty-five small fish with tomato sauce, and four portions of tripe with Parmesan cheese. And because she thought the tripe was not seasoned enough, she asked three times for the butter and grated cheese!

The fox, too, would gladly have nibbled a little, but his doctor had put him on a strict diet, so he was forced to be content with simply a hare dressed with sweet and sour sauce, garnished lightly with fat chickens and young hens. After the hare, he sent for a casserole of partridges, rabbits, frogs, lizards, and other delicacies, but he would not touch anything else. He was so disgusted by the sight of food, he said, that he could put nothing more to his lips.

The one who ate the least was Pinocchio. He asked for some walnuts and bread, but he left everything on his plate. The poor boy, whose thoughts were fixed on the Field of

Miracles, had gotten a case of mental indigestion just thinking about the gold pieces.

After supper, the fox said to the innkeeper, "Give us two good rooms, one for Mr. Pinocchio, and the other for me and my companion. We will catch a little sleep before we leave. Remember, however, that at midnight we wish to be called to continue our journey."

"Yes, gentlemen," answered the innkeeper, and he winked at the fox and the cat as if to say, "I know what you're up to. We understand one another!"

As soon as Pinocchio got into bed, he fell asleep and began to dream. He dreamed that he was in the middle of a field, and the field was full of shrubs covered with clusters of gold pieces that clinked in the wind as if to say, "Whoever wants us, come and take us." But when Pinocchio was at the most interesting moment—that is, just as he was stretching out his hand to pick handfuls of those beautiful gold pieces and put them in his pocket—he was awakened suddenly by three violent knocks on the door of his room.

It was the innkeeper, who had come to tell him that midnight had struck.

"Are my companions ready?" asked the puppet.

"Ready? Why, they left two hours ago."

"Why were they in such a hurry?"

"Because the cat received a message that her eldest kitten was ill with swollen feet, and was in danger of dying."

"Did they pay for the supper?"

"What a question! They are too well-educated to dream of offering such an insult to a gentleman like you."

"What a pity! It's an insult that would have given me much pleasure!" said Pinocchio, scratching his head. He then asked, "And where did my good friends say they would wait for me?"

"At the Field of Miracles, tomorrow morning, at daybreak."

Pinocchio paid for his supper and that of his companions with a gold piece and left.

It was so pitch dark outside the inn that the puppet could not even see his hand in front of his face and had to grope his way along. In the surrounding countryside, not a leaf moved. Some night birds, flying across the road from one hedge to the other, brushed Pinocchio's nose with their wings as they passed, which frightened him so that he jumped back, shouting, "Who goes there?" The echo in the surrounding hills responded, "Who goes there? Who goes there? Who goes there?"

As he walked on, he saw a little insect shining dimly on the trunk of a tree, like a nightlight with a shade of transparent china.

"Who are you?" asked Pinocchio.

"I am the ghost of the talking cricket," answered the insect in a low voice so weak and faint that it seemed to come from another world.

"What do you want with me?" said the puppet.

"I want to give you some advice. Go back home, and take the four gold pieces that you have left to your poor father, who is weeping with despair because you have not returned to him."

"Tomorrow my father will be a rich gentleman, for these four gold pieces will have become two thousand."

"My boy, don't put your trust in those who promise to make you rich in a day. Usually they are either fools or scoundrels! Listen to me, and go back."

"No, I'm determined to go on."

"The hour is late!"

"I'm determined to go on."

"The night is dark!"

"I'm determined to go on."

"The road is dangerous!"

"I'm determined to go on."

"Remember that children who are determined to do as they please and have their own way regret it sooner or later."

"Always the same stories. Good night, cricket."

"Good night, Pinocchio, and may Heaven save you from dangers and assassins."

With these words, the talking cricket vanished suddenly, like a light that has been blown out, and the road became darker than ever.

{ Chapter 14 }

The puppet falls among assassins

Really," said the puppet to himself as he resumed his journey, "how unfortunate we poor children are. Everybody scolds us, everybody admonishes us, everybody gives us advice. The way they talk, they think they are our fathers and our masters—every one of them, even the talking cricket! Just imagine: because I chose not to listen to that tiresome cricket, who knows how many misfortunes are to happen to me! I'll even meet assassins! That matters little, though, for I don't believe in assassins—I've never believed in them. I think that assassins were invented by fathers to frighten boys who want to go out at night. Besides, suppose I was to come across them here in the road. Do you think they would frighten me? Not in the least. I would walk up to them and say, 'Gentlemen assassins, what do you want with me? Remember that with me there is no joking. Go about your business and be quiet!' If those poor assassins heard me speaking in that determined way, they would run away like the wind. If they didn't run away, why, then I would run away myself, and that would be the end of it."

But Pinocchio did not have time to finish his reasoning, because at that moment he heard a slight rustling of leaves behind him.

He turned quickly to look, and saw in the gloom two evil-looking black figures completely covered in coal sacks. They were running after him on tiptoe, and making great leaps like two phantoms.

"Here they are in reality!" he said to himself, and not knowing where to hide his gold pieces, he put them in his mouth, under his tongue.

Then he tried to escape. But before he could take a step, he was seized by the arm and heard two horrid voices saying to him, "Your money or your life!"

Pinocchio, not being able to answer in words, because of the money in his mouth, made a thousand low bows and gestures to make the two cloaked figures, whose eyes were visible only through holes in their sacks, understand that he was a poor puppet, and that he had not so much as a counterfeit coin in his pocket.

"Come now! Less nonsense and out with the money!" cried the two bandits threateningly.

And the puppet made a gesture with his hands as if to say, "I don't have any."

"Hand over your money or you are dead," said the taller of the bandits.

"Dead!" repeated the other.

"And after we kill you, we'll kill your father, too."

"Your father!"

"No, no, no, not my poor father!" cried Pinocchio in a despairing tone. As he said it, the gold pieces clinked in his mouth.

"Ah! You rascal! You've hidden the money under your tongue! Spit it out at once!"

But Pinocchio did not obey.

"Ah! You pretend to be deaf, do you? Wait a moment and we'll find a means to make you spit it out."

One of them seized the puppet by the end of his nose, and the other took him by the chin, and they began to pull brutally, one up and the other down, to force him to open his mouth, but it was no use. Pinocchio's mouth seemed to be nailed and riveted shut.

Then the shorter assassin drew out an ugly knife and tried to force it between Pinocchio's lips like a lever or chisel. But Pinocchio, quick as lightning, caught the assassin's hand with his teeth, bit it clean off, and spat it out. Imagine his astonishment when he saw that he had spat a cat's paw, not a hand, onto the ground!

Encouraged by this first victory, Pinocchio gave such a sudden twist that he freed himself from his assailants and, jumping the hedge by the road, began to dash across the countryside. The assassins ran after him like two dogs chasing a hare. The one who had lost a paw ran on one leg, though goodness knows how he did it.

After a race of many miles, Pinocchio could go no farther. Giving himself up for lost, he climbed the trunk of a very tall pine tree and sat in the upper branches. The assassins attempted to climb after him, but halfway up the trunk, they slid down, landing on the ground with skinned hands and feet.

But they were not to be beaten so easily. They collected some dry wood, piled it beneath the pine, and set fire to it. In no time at all the pine began to burn and flame like a candle blown by the wind. Pinocchio, seeing the flames mounting higher every instant, and not wanting to end his life like a roasted pigeon, made a spectacular leap from the top of the tree and started running across the fields and vineyards. The assassins followed close behind him without slowing.

When day broke, they were still pursuing him. Suddenly Pinocchio found his way barred by a wide, deep ditch full of dirty water the color of coffee. What was he to do? "One! Two! Three!" cried the puppet, and making a rush, he sprang to the other side. The assassins also jumped, but not having measured the distance properly—splash! splash!—they fell right in the middle of the ditch. Pinocchio, who heard the splashing water, laughed and shouted, "A fine bath to you, gentlemen assassins!"

Pinocchio was sure they were drowned, when, turning to look, he saw they were both running after him, still enveloped in their sacks, water dripping from them as if they had each sprung a leak.

{ Chapter 15 }

Pinocchio is hanged

t this sight, the puppet's courage failed him, and he was on the verge of throwing himself on the ground and giving up. However, turning his eyes in every direction, he saw at some distance a small house as white as snow, standing out amidst the dark green of the trees.

"If only I had enough breath to reach that house," he said to himself, "perhaps I'd be saved."

Without delaying an instant, he ran for his life through the woods, the assassins close behind him.

At last, after a desperate race of nearly two hours, he arrived quite breathless at the door of the house.

He knocked, but no one answered.

He knocked again, much louder, for he heard the sound of footsteps approaching, and the heavy panting of his pursuers. The same silence as before.

Seeing that it was useless to knock, he began in desperation to kick and pound the door with all his might. Suddenly the window opened, and a beautiful child appeared. She had blue hair and a face as white as a waxen image; her eyes were closed and her hands were crossed on her breast. Without moving her lips, she said in a voice that

seemed to come from another world, "In this house there is no one. They are all dead."

"Then at least open the door for me yourself," cried Pinocchio pleadingly.

"I'm dead, too."

"Dead? Then what are you doing at the window?"

"I'm waiting for my coffin to come and carry me away."

Having said this, she immediately disappeared, and the window closed without the slightest noise.

"Oh! Beautiful child with blue hair," said Pinocchio, "open the door for pity's sake! Have compassion on a poor boy pursued by assas—"

But before he could finish, he was seized by the collar, and the same two horrible voices said to him threateningly, "You won't escape from us again!"

The puppet, fearing that his end was near, trembled so violently that the joints of his wooden legs began to creak, and the gold pieces hidden under his tongue clinked.

"Now then," demanded the assassins, "will you open your mouth? Yes or no? Ah! No answer? Leave it to us. This time we'll force you to open it!"

And drawing out two long, horrid knives as sharp as razors—slash! slash!—they attempted to stab him twice.

But the puppet, luckily for him, was made of very hard wood. The knife blades broke into a thousand pieces, and the assassins were left with only the handles in their hands, staring at each other.

"I see what we must do," said one of them. "He must be hanged! Let's hang him!"

"Hang him!" repeated the other.

Without wasting any time, they tied Pinocchio's arms behind him, slipped a noose around his neck, and hung him from the branch of a tree called the Big Oak.

They then sat down on the ground and waited for his last struggle. But after three hours, the puppet's eyes were still open, his mouth closed, and he was kicking more than ever.

Losing patience, the assassins said to Pinocchio, "Good-bye 'til tomorrow. Let's

hope that when we return you will be polite enough to be found quite dead, and with your mouth wide open."

And off they walked.

In the meantime, a tempestuous northerly wind began to blow, and it beat the poor puppet from side to side, making him swing violently like the clapper of a bell ringing for a wedding. The swinging hurt him terribly, and the noose, becoming still tighter around his throat, took away his breath.

Little by little, his eyes began to grow dim, but even though he felt that death was near, he continued to hope that some charitable person would come to his assistance before it was too late. But when, after waiting and waiting, he found that no one came, he remembered his poor father, and thinking he was dying, he stammered, "Oh, Father! Father! If only you were here!"

His breath failed him, and he could say no more. He shut his eyes, opened his mouth, stretched his legs, gave a long shudder, and hung stiff.

{ Chapter 16 }

The beautiful child with blue hair

hile poor Pinocchio, suspended from a branch of the Big Oak, was apparently more dead than alive, the beautiful child with the blue hair came again to the window. When she saw the unhappy puppet hanging by his neck, and dancing up and down in the gusts of the north wind, she was moved by compassion. She quietly clapped her hands three times.

At this signal there came a sound of the sweeping of wings, and a large falcon flew to the windowsill.

"What are your orders, gracious fairy?" he asked, bowing his beak as a sign of reverence—for I must tell you that the child with the blue hair was in fact a beautiful fairy who had lived in the woods for more than a thousand years.

"Do you see that puppet dangling from a branch of the Big Oak?"

"I see him."

"Very well. Fly there at once. With your strong beak, break the knot that keeps him suspended in the air, and then lay him gently on the ground at the foot of the tree."

The falcon flew away, and after two minutes he returned, saying, "I have done as you commanded."

"And how did you find him—alive or dead?"

"He appeared dead, but he can't really be dead, for I had no sooner loosened the noose around his throat than he muttered in a faint voice, 'Now I feel better!'"

The fairy clapped her hands twice, and a magnificent poodle appeared, walking upright on his hind legs, exactly as if he were a man.

He was dressed as a coachman. He wore a three-cornered cap braided with gold, a curly white wig that came down to his shoulders, and a chocolate-colored vest with diamond buttons and two large pockets to hold the bones that his mistress gave him at dinner. He also wore a pair of crimson velvet breeches, silk stockings, short boots, and a kind of umbrella case made of blue satin, in which to put his tail when the weather was stormy.

"Be quick, Medoro, like a good dog!" said the fairy to the poodle. "Have the most beautiful carriage in my coach house readied and take the road to the woods. When you come to the Big Oak, you'll find a poor puppet stretched out on the ground half dead. Pick him up gently and lay him on the cushions of the carriage. Bring him here to me. Have you understood?"

The poodle, to show that he had

understood, shook the case of blue satin on his tail three or four times and ran off like a racehorse.

Shortly afterwards, a beautiful little carriage came out of the coach house. Its cushions were stuffed with canary feathers, and the inside was lined with whipped cream, custard, and sweet biscuits. The little carriage was drawn by a hundred pairs of white mice, and the poodle, seated on the coach box, cracked his whip from side to side like a driver afraid of being late.

Less than a quarter hour later, the carriage returned. The fairy, who was waiting at the door of the house, took the poor puppet in her arms and carried him into a little room that was lined with mother-of-pearl. She then sent at once for the most famous doctors in the neighborhood.

The doctors came immediately, one right after the other: the first a crow, another an owl, and the third a talking cricket.

"I wish to know from you gentlemen," said the fairy, turning to the three doctors assembled around Pinocchio's bed, "if this unfortunate puppet is alive or dead!"

The crow, coming forward first, felt Pinocchio's pulse, then his nose, and then the little toe of his foot. Having done this carefully, he solemnly declared, "In my opinion, the puppet is already quite dead. But if, unfortunately, he should not be dead, then it would be a sure sign that he is still alive!"

"I regret," said the owl, "that I must contradict the crow, my illustrious friend and colleague. In my opinion, the puppet is still alive. If, unfortunately, he should not be alive, then it would be a sure sign that he is dead!"

"And you—have you nothing to say?" asked the fairy of the talking cricket.

"In my opinion, the wisest thing a prudent doctor can do, when he doesn't know what he is talking about, is to be silent. Furthermore, this puppet has a face that is not new to me. I have known him for some time!"

Pinocchio, who up to that moment had lain lifeless, like a real piece of wood, was seized with a fit of convulsive trembling that shook the whole bed.

"That puppet there," continued the talking cricket, "is a perfect rogue."

Pinocchio opened his eyes, but shut them again quickly.

"He is a beggar, a do-nothing, a vagabond."

Pinocchio hid his face beneath the sheets.

"That puppet there is a disobedient son who will make his poor father die of a broken heart!"

At that instant, the muffled sounds of sobbing and crying were heard in the room. Imagine everybody's surprise when, having raised the sheets a little, it was discovered that the sounds came from Pinocchio.

"When a dead person cries, it's a sign that he is on the road to getting well," said the crow solemnly.

"I am sorry to contradict my illustrious friend and colleague," added the owl, "but in my opinion, when a live person cries, it's a sign that he does not want to die."

{ Chapter 17 }

Pinocchio eats some sugar and tells a lie

s soon as the three doctors had left the room, the fairy approached Pinocchio and, touching his forehead, perceived that he had a dangerous fever.

She therefore dissolved some white powder in half a glass of water and offered it to the puppet, saying gently, "Drink it, and in a few days you will be better."

Pinocchio looked at the glass, made a sour face, and asked in a whining voice, "Is it sweet or bitter?"

"It's bitter, but it will do you good."

"If it's bitter, I won't take it."

"Listen to me, and drink it."

"I don't like anything bitter."

"Drink it, and when you have, I'll give you a lump of sugar to take away the taste."

"Where is the lump of sugar?"

"Here it is," said the fairy, taking a piece from a gold sugar bowl.

"Give me the lump of sugar first, and then I'll drink that bad, bitter water."

"Do you promise?"

"Yes."

The fairy gave him the sugar, and Pinocchio, having crunched it up and swallowed it in a second, said, licking his lips, "It would be a fine thing if sugar was medicine! I'd take it every day."

"Now keep your promise and drink these few drops of water, which will restore your health."

Pinocchio took the glass unwillingly in his hand and put the point of his nose to it. He then brought the glass to his lips. He then again put his nose to it, and at last said, "It's too bitter! Too bitter! I can't drink it."

"How do you know that, when you haven't even tasted it?"

"I can imagine it! I know it from the smell. I want another lump of sugar, and then I'll drink it."

With all the patience of a good mother, the fairy put another lump of sugar in his mouth, and again handed him the glass.

"I can't drink it like this!" said the puppet, making a thousand grimaces.

"Why?"

"Because that pillow on my feet bothers me."

The fairy removed the pillow.

"It's useless. I still can't drink it."

"What's wrong now?"

"The door is half open. That bothers me."

The fairy went and closed the door.

"The fact is," cried Pinocchio, bursting into tears, "I won't drink that bitter water—no, no, no!"

"My boy, you'll be sorry."

"I don't care."

"Your illness is serious."

"I don't care."

"The fever will carry you into the other world in a few hours."

"I don't care."

"Aren't you afraid to die?"

"I'm not afraid in the least! I'd rather die than drink that bitter medicine."

At that moment, the door of the room flew open, and four rabbits as black as ink entered, carrying a little coffin on their shoulders.

"What do you want with me?" cried Pinocchio, sitting up in terror.

"We've come to take you," said the biggest rabbit.

"To take me? But I'm not dead yet!"

"No, not yet. But you have only a few minutes to live, as you have refused the medicine that would cure you of the fever."

"Oh, fairy, fairy!" the puppet cried. "Give me the glass at once! And be quick, for pity's sake! I don't want to die! No, I will not die!"

He took the glass in both hands and emptied it in one gulp.

"We must have patience!" said the rabbits. "This time we've made our journey in vain." And lifting the little coffin back onto their shoulders, they left the room, grumbling and murmuring.

A few moments later, Pinocchio jumped down from the bed quite well, for you see, wooden puppets have the privilege of being seldom ill and of being cured very quickly.

When the fairy saw him running and rushing about the room as happy and lively as a young rooster, she said to him, "Then my medicine has really done you good?"

"Good? I should think so! It has restored me to life!"

"Then why on earth did you require so much persuasion to take it?"

"Because we boys are all like that! We're more afraid of the medicine than of the illness."

"Disgraceful! Children ought to know that a good remedy taken in time may save them from a serious illness, and perhaps even death."

"Oh, but next time I won't require so much persuasion. I'll remember those black rabbits with the coffin on their shoulders. And then I'll immediately take the glass in my hand, and down it will go!"

"Now, come here, and tell me how it came to be that you fell into the hands of those assassins."

"It started when the Showman, Fire-Eater, gave me some gold pieces and said, 'Go, and take them to your father!' and instead I met on the road a fox and a cat, two very respectable people, who said to me, 'Would you like those pieces of gold to become a thousand or two? Come with us, and we'll take you to the Field of Miracles,' and I said, 'Let's go!' And they said, 'Let's stop at the Lobster Inn first,' and after midnight they left. When I awoke, I found that they were no longer there, because they had gone away. Then I began to travel by night, and you can't imagine how dark it was! I met on the road two assassins in coal sacks who said, 'Out with your money,' and I said, 'I have none,' because I had hidden the four gold pieces in my mouth, and one of the assassins tried to put his hand in my mouth, and I bit off his hand and spat it out, but instead of a hand, I spat out a cat's paw. And the assassins ran after me, and I ran and ran until at last they caught me, and tied me by the neck to a tree in this woods, and said, 'Tomorrow we will return, and then you'll be dead, with your mouth open, and we'll be able to carry off the pieces of gold that you've hidden under your tongue.'"

"And the four pieces—where have you put them?" asked the fairy.

"I've lost them!" said Pinocchio. But he was telling a lie, for he had them in his pocket.

He had scarcely told the lie when his nose, which was already long, grew at once two fingers longer.

"And where did you lose them?"

"In the woods near here."

At this second lie, his nose grew even longer.

"If you've lost them in the woods near here," said the fairy, "we'll look for them, and we'll find them, because everything that is lost in that woods is always found."

"Ah! Now I remember," replied the puppet. "I didn't lose the four gold pieces. I swallowed them by mistake while I was drinking your medicine."

At this third lie, his nose grew to such an extraordinary length that poor Pinocchio could not move in any direction. If he turned to one side, he struck his nose against the bed or the windowpane. If he turned to the other, he struck it against the wall or the door. If he raised his head a little, he ran the risk of putting it in the fairy's eyes.

The fairy looked at him and laughed.

"What are you laughing at?" asked the puppet, very confused and worried about his nose growing to such great lengths.

"I'm laughing at the lies you've told."

"How can you possibly know that I've been telling lies?"

"Lies, my dear boy, are found out immediately, because they are of two sorts. There are lies that have short legs, and lies that have long noses. Your lies, as it happens, have long noses."

Pinocchio, not knowing where to hide himself for shame, tried to run out of the room; but he did not succeed, for his nose had grown so much that it could no longer pass through the door.

❧

{ Chapter 18 }

The Field of Miracles

he fairy, as you may imagine, allowed the puppet to cry and howl for a good half-hour over his nose. This she did to teach him a lesson, and to correct him of the disgraceful habit of telling lies—the most disgraceful habit that a child can have. But when she saw him, his eyes swollen from weeping, she was filled with compassion and clapped her hands. At that signal a thousand woodpeckers flew in the window. They immediately perched on Pinocchio's nose and began to peck at it with such zeal that in a few minutes his enormous and ridiculous nose was reduced to its usual dimensions.

"What a good fairy you are," said the puppet, drying his eyes, "and how much I love you!"

"I love you, too," answered the fairy, "and if you want to stay with me, you'll be my little brother, and I'll be your good sister."

"I would stay willingly, but what about my poor father?"

"I've thought of everything, and your father already knows everything. He will be here tonight."

"Really?" shouted Pinocchio, jumping for joy. "Then, dear fairy, with your permission, I would like to go and meet him. I'm so anxious to give a kiss to that poor old man who has suffered so much on my account."

"Go, then, but be careful not to lose your way. Take the road through the woods, and I'm sure that you will meet him."

Pinocchio set out, and as soon as he was in the woods, he began to run like a deer. But when he reached a certain spot almost in front of the Big Oak, he stopped, for he heard people among the bushes. Can you guess who they were? Yes, it was his two traveling companions, the fox and the cat, with whom he had eaten dinner at the Lobster Inn.

"Why, here is our dear Pinocchio!" cried the fox, kissing and embracing him. "What brings you here?"

"What brings you here?" repeated the cat.

"It's a long story," answered the puppet, "which I'll tell you when I have time. But you should know that the other night, when you left me alone at the inn, I met with assassins on the road."

"Assassins! Oh, poor Pinocchio! And what did they want?"

"They wanted to rob me of my gold pieces."

"Villains!" said the fox.

"Infamous villains!" repeated the cat.

"But I ran away from them," continued the puppet, "and they followed me, and at last they overtook me and hung me from a branch of that oak tree."

"Is it possible to hear of anything more dreadful?" said the fox. "What a world we are condemned to live in! Where can respectable people like us find a safe refuge?"

While they were talking, Pinocchio noticed that the cat's front right leg was lame, for she had lost her paw. He therefore asked her, "What's happened to your paw?"

The cat tried to answer but became confused. So the fox immediately interrupted, "My friend is too modest, and that's why she doesn't speak. I'll answer for her. I must tell you that an hour ago we met an old wolf on the road, who was almost fainting from hunger. He asked food of us, but not having so much as a fishbone to give him, what did my friend, who has the heart of a saint, do? She bit off one of her forepaws and threw it to that poor beast so he might satisfy his hunger."

And the fox, as he said this, wiped away a tear.

Pinocchio was also touched and said to the cat, "If all cats were as kind as you, how fortunate the mice would be!"

"And now, what are you doing here?" asked the fox of the puppet.

"I'm waiting for my father, whom I expect to arrive at any moment."

"And your gold pieces?"

"I have them in my pocket—except the one that I spent at the Lobster Inn."

"And to think that those four pieces might become one or two thousand by tomorrow! Why don't you listen to my advice? Why not go and bury them in the Field of Miracles?"

"It's impossible today. I'll go another day."

"Another day will be too late!" said the fox.

"Why?"

"Because the field has been bought by a gentleman, and after tomorrow no one will be allowed to bury money there."

"How far away is the Field of Miracles?"

"Not even two miles. Will you come with us? In half an hour you'll be there. You can bury your money at once, and in a few minutes you'll collect two thousand coins, and this evening you'll return with your pockets full. Will you come?"

Pinocchio thought of the good fairy, old Geppetto, and the warning of the talking cricket, and he hesitated a little before answering. In the end, however, he did as all boys do who have not a grain of sense and who have no heart—he gave his head a little nod and said to the fox and the cat, "Let's go! I'll come with you."

So off they went.

After having walked half the day, they reached a town called Fools' Trap. As soon as Pinocchio entered the town, he saw that the streets were crowded with dogs who had lost their coats and were yawning from hunger; shorn sheep, trembling with cold; roosters without combs or crests who were begging for a grain of corn; large butterflies who could no longer fly because they had sold their beautifully colored wings;

peacocks who had no tails and were ashamed to be seen; and pheasants who went scratching about in a subdued fashion, mourning for their brilliant gold and silver feathers, gone forever.

In the midst of this crowd of beggars and shame-faced creatures, a fine carriage passed from time to time, carrying a fox, or a thieving magpie, or some other ravenous bird of prey.

"And where is the Field of Miracles?" asked Pinocchio.

"Right here, not but a few steps away from us."

They crossed the town, and having gone beyond the walls, they came to a solitary field that looked just like any other field.

"We've arrived," said the fox to the puppet. "Now, stoop down and dig a little hole in the ground with your hands and put your gold pieces into it."

Pinocchio obeyed. He dug a hole, put the four gold pieces into it, and filled up the hole with dirt.

"Now, then," said the fox, "go to that canal close to us, fetch a pail of water, and water the ground where you have sowed your gold."

Pinocchio went to the canal, but since he had no pail, he took off one of his old shoes, filled it with water, and then watered the ground over his gold pieces.

"Is there anything else to be done?" the puppet asked.

"Nothing else," answered the fox. "We can now go away. You can return in about twenty minutes, and you'll find a shrub already pushing through the ground, with its branches quite loaded with money."

The poor puppet, beside himself with joy, thanked the fox and the cat a thousand times, and promised them a beautiful present.

"We wish for no presents," they answered. "It is enough for us to have taught you the way to get rich without hard work. That makes us very happy."

Having said this, they bid farewell to Pinocchio, wished him a good harvest, and went about their business.

⚜

{ Chapter 19 }

Pinocchio is robbed

he puppet returned to the town and began to count the minutes one by one. And when he thought that it must be time, he ran back to the Field of Miracles.

He ran as fast as he could, his heart beating like a grandfather clock—*tick, tock, tick, tock*. All the while he was thinking, "What if instead of a thousand gold pieces, I find two thousand on the branches of the tree? Or instead of two thousand, suppose I find five thousand? Or instead of five thousand, what if I find a hundred thousand? Oh! What a fine gentleman I should become then! I would have a beautiful palace, a thousand little wooden horses and a thousand stables to amuse myself with, a cellar full of sweet syrups, and a library full of candies, tarts, plum cakes, macaroons, and biscuits with cream."

While he was building these castles in the sky, he came near the field and stopped to see if he could catch a glimpse of a tree laden with money, but he saw nothing. He went another thirty steps—nothing. He entered the field and went right up to the little hole where he had buried his gold pieces—nothing. He took his hands out of his pockets and gave his head a long scratch.

Suddenly, he heard an explosion of laughter nearby. Looking up he saw a large parrot perched on a tree, pruning the few feathers he had left.

"Why are you laughing?" asked Pinocchio angrily.

"I'm laughing because while pruning my feathers, I tickled myself under my wings."

The puppet did not answer. He went to the canal, filled the same old shoe full of water, and again watered the earth that covered his gold pieces.

While he was occupied, another laugh, more impertinent than the first, rang out in the silence of that solitary place.

"Once and for all," shouted Pinocchio in a rage, "tell me, you ill-educated parrot, what are you laughing at?"

"I'm laughing at those simpletons who believe in all the foolish things they hear, and who allow themselves to be entrapped by those who are more cunning than they."

"Are you, perhaps, speaking of me?"

"Yes, I'm speaking of you, poor Pinocchio—of you who are simple enough to believe that money can be sown and gathered in fields like beans and squash. I also believed it once, and today I'm suffering because of it. Today—alas, it's too late— I have at last learned that to put a few pennies together honestly, it's necessary to know how to earn them, either by the work of your own hands or by the cleverness of your own brain."

"I don't understand," said the puppet, who was already trembling with fear.

"Have patience! I'll explain myself better," said the parrot. "You must know that while you were in town, the fox and the cat returned to the field. They took the buried money and then fled like the wind. And no one will be able to catch them now."

Pinocchio stood with his mouth open and, choosing not to believe the parrot's words, began to dig up the earth he had watered. He dug, and dug, and dug, and made such a deep hole that a shock of corn might have stood upright in it. But the money was no longer there.

In a state of desperation, he rushed back to the town and went at once to the Court of Justice to denounce the two thieves who had robbed him.

The judge was an old gorilla who looked most respectable on account of his age, his white beard, and the gold spectacles without lenses that he had to wear because of an inflammation of the eyes that had tormented him for many years.

Pinocchio told the judge all the particulars of the infamous fraud of which he had been the victim. He gave the names, the surnames, and other details of the two rascals, and concluded by demanding justice.

The judge listened with great kindness, took a lively interest in the story, and was very moved. And when the puppet had nothing further to say, the judge stretched out his hand and rang a bell.

At this summons, two mastiffs immediately appeared, dressed as policemen. The judge, pointing to Pinocchio, said to them, "This poor devil has been robbed of four gold pieces. Arrest him and put him in prison immediately."

The puppet was petrified upon hearing this unexpected sentence and tried to protest, but the policemen clamped his mouth shut and carried him off to jail.

And there he remained for four months—four long months—and he would have remained longer still if a fortunate chance had not released him.

As it happened, the young emperor who reigned over the town of Fools' Trap, having won a splendid victory over his enemies, ordered a great public celebration. There were fireworks, horse races, and bicycle races, and as a further sign of triumph, he commanded that the jails be opened and all the prisoners set free.

"If the others are to be let out of prison, I ought to be let out, too," said Pinocchio to the jailer.

"No, not you," said the jailer, "because you don't belong to that class of people."

"I beg your pardon," replied Pinocchio. "I'm a criminal, too!"

"In that case, you're perfectly right," said the jailer, and taking off his hat and bowing to him respectfully, he opened the prison door and let the puppet go.

⁂

{ Chapter 20 }

Pinocchio sets out for the fairy's house

magine Pinocchio's joy when he found himself free. Without stopping to take a breath, he immediately left the town and took the road that led to the fairy's house.

On account of rainy weather, the road had become a marsh into which the puppet sank knee-deep. But he would not give up. Spurred on by the desire to see his father and his sister with blue hair again, he ran and leaped like a greyhound, and as he ran, he was splashed with mud from head to foot. And he said to himself as he went along, "How many misfortunes have happened to me—and I have deserved them! For I'm an obstinate, willful puppet. I'm always determined to have my own way, without listening to those who wish me well, and who have a thousand times more sense than I! But from this time forth, I'm determined to change and to become orderly and obedient. For at last I've seen that disobedient boys come to no good and gain nothing. And will my father have waited for me? Will I find him at the fairy's house? Poor man, it's so long since I last saw him. I'm dying to embrace him and cover him with kisses! And will the fairy forgive me for disobeying her? To think of all the kindness and loving care I received from her—to think that I'm now alive because of her! Would it be possible to find a more ungrateful boy, or one with less heart than I?"

Upon saying these last few words, he stopped suddenly, frightened to death, and took four steps backwards.

What had he seen?

He saw an immense serpent stretched across the road. Its skin was green, it had red eyes, and its pointed tail smoked like a chimney.

It would be impossible to imagine the puppet's terror. He walked away to a safe distance, sat down on a pile of stones, and waited for the serpent to go about its business and leave the road clear.

He waited an hour—two hours—three hours—but the serpent stayed there, and even from a distance Pinocchio could see the red light of its fiery eyes and the column of smoke that ascended from the end of its tail.

At last, Pinocchio, trying to feel courageous, approached to within a few steps and said to the serpent in a little, soft voice, "Excuse me, Mr. Serpent, but would you be so good as to move a little to one side, just enough to allow me to pass?"

He might as well have spoken to a wall. The serpent did not move.

He began again in the same soft voice, "You must know, Mr. Serpent, that I'm on my way home, where my father is waiting for me, and it's such a long time since I last saw him! Will you allow me to continue on my way?"

He waited for some sign in answer to this request, but there was none. In fact, the serpent, who until that moment had been sprightly and full of life, became motionless and almost rigid. It shut its eyes, and its tail stopped smoking.

"Can it really be dead?" asked Pinocchio, rubbing his hands with delight. But just as he was going to leap over its body to reach the other side of the road, the serpent suddenly rose on end, like a spring set in motion, and the puppet, in his terror, drew back, caught his feet, and fell to the ground.

He fell so awkwardly that his head stuck in the mud, and his legs went into the air.

At the sight of the puppet kicking violently, with his head in the mud, the serpent was seized by a fit of laughter, and it laughed, and laughed, and laughed, until it broke a blood vessel and died. And this time, it really was dead.

Pinocchio set off running in hopes that he would reach the fairy's house before dark. But before long he began to suffer so dreadfully from hunger that he could not bear it, so he jumped into a field by the wayside, intending to pick some bunches of grapes. Oh, that he had never done that!

Pinocchio had barely reached the vines when—*crack!*—his legs were caught between two sets of sharp iron teeth. The pain was so terrible that stars of every color danced before his eyes. The poor puppet had been caught in a trap put there to catch some big weasels who had been terrorizing the poultry yards in the neighborhood.

{ *Chapter 21* }

The peasant and his watchdog

inocchio, as you might imagine, began to cry and scream. But his tears and groans were useless, for there was not a house to be seen, and not a living soul passed down the road.

At last night came.

Partly from the pain of the trap that cut his legs, and partly from fear at finding himself alone in the dark fields, the puppet was on the verge of fainting. Just then, a firefly flitted over his head. He called to it and asked, "Oh, little firefly, will you have pity on me and free me from this torture?"

"Poor boy!" said the firefly, who stopped and looked at him with compassion. "How did you ever get your legs caught in those sharp iron teeth?"

"I came into the field to pick some grapes, and—"

"But were the grapes yours?"

"No."

"Then who taught you to take other people's property?"

"I was so hungry."

"Hunger, my boy, is not a good reason for taking what does not belong to you."

"That's true, that's true," said Pinocchio, crying. "I'll never do it again."

At this moment their conversation was interrupted by the sound of approaching

footsteps. It was the owner of the field, coming on tiptoe to see if one of the weasels that was eating his chickens during the night had been caught in his trap.

Imagine his surprise when, having brought out his lantern from under his coat, he saw that he had caught a puppet instead of a weasel!

"Ah, little thief!" said the angry peasant. "So it's you who carries off my chickens?"

"No, it's not I! Indeed it's not!" cried Pinocchio, sobbing. "I only came into the field to pick some grapes!"

"He who steals grapes is quite capable of stealing chickens. Leave it to me; I'll teach you a lesson that you won't soon forget."

The man opened the trap, seized the puppet by the collar, and carried him to his house as if he was a lamb.

When he reached the yard in front of the house, he threw Pinocchio roughly on the ground, put his foot on the puppet's neck, and said, "It's late, and I want to go to bed. We'll settle our accounts tomorrow. In the meantime, as the dog who kept guard at night died today, you will take his place. You will be my watchdog."

With that, the peasant took a great collar covered with brass knobs and strapped it tightly around the puppet's throat so that he could not draw his head out. A heavy chain, attached to the collar, was fastened to the wall.

"If it should rain tonight," the man said, "you can go and lie down in the kennel. The straw that has served as a bed for my poor dog for the last four years is still there. Remember to keep your ears open. And if the robbers should come, bark!"

After giving these instructions, the man went into the house, shut the door, and locked it.

Poor Pinocchio lay on the ground more dead than alive from the effects of cold, hunger, and fear. From time to time he put his hands angrily to the collar that pinched his throat and said, crying, "It serves me right! It certainly serves me right! I was determined to be a vagabond and a good-for-nothing. I listened to bad companions, and that's why I have always met with misfortune. If I had been a good little boy, if I had been willing to learn and to work, if I had remained at home with my poor father, I would not be in the middle of a field, working as a watchdog for a peasant. Oh, how I wish that I could be born again! But now it's too late, and I must have patience!"

Relieved by this little outburst, which came straight from his heart, he went into the dog kennel and fell asleep.

{ Chapter 22 }

Pinocchio catches the thieves

✦

He had been sleeping heavily for about two hours when, around midnight, he was roused by a whispering of strange voices that seemed to come from the courtyard. Poking the point of his nose out of the kennel, he saw four little cat-like beasts with dark fur, standing together. But they were not cats; they were weasels—carnivorous little animals who are especially fond of eggs and young chickens. One of the weasels, leaving his companions, came to the opening of the kennel and said in a low voice, "Good evening, Melampo."

"My name is not Melampo," answered the puppet.

"Oh! Then who are you?"

"I'm Pinocchio."

"And what are you doing here?"

"I'm acting as watchdog."

"But where is Melampo? Where is the old dog who lived in this kennel?"

"He died this morning."

"He's dead? Poor beast! He was so good. But judging by your face, I should say that you are also a good dog."

"I beg your pardon, but I'm not a dog."

"Not a dog? Then what are you?"

"I'm a puppet."

"And you're acting as watchdog?"

"Yes—as punishment."

"Well, then, I'll offer you the same conditions that we made with the deceased Melampo, and I'm sure you will be satisfied with them."

"What are these conditions?"

"One night every week you will let us visit this poultry yard and carry off eight chickens. Of these chickens, seven are to be eaten by us, and one we'll give to you, with the understanding, however, that you pretend to be asleep, and that you never bark or wake the peasant."

"Is that what Melampo did?" asked Pinocchio.

"Certainly, and we were always on the best of terms with him. Sleep quietly, and rest assured that before we go, we'll leave by the kennel a beautiful chicken, already plucked, for your breakfast tomorrow. Do we understand each other?"

"Only too clearly!" answered Pinocchio, but with a look that seemed to say, "We'll soon see about that!"

The four weasels, thinking themselves safe, crept to the poultry yard, which was close to the kennel, opened the wooden gate with their teeth and claws, and slipped in one by one. But they had only just passed through when they heard the gate shut behind them with a loud bang.

It was Pinocchio who had shut it, and for greater security he put a large stone against the door to keep it closed.

He then began to bark, and he barked exactly like a watchdog: "Bow-wow! Bow-wow!"

Upon hearing the barking, the peasant jumped out of bed, grabbed his gun, and came to the window, calling, "What's the matter?"

"There are robbers!" answered Pinocchio.

"Where are they?"

"In the poultry yard."

"I'll come right down!"

In less time than it takes to say "Amen," the peasant was there. He rushed into the poultry yard, caught the weasels, put them into a sack, and said to them with great satisfaction, "At last you have fallen into my hands! I should punish you, but I'm not so cruel. I will be content instead to carry you in the morning to the innkeeper of the neighboring village, who will skin and cook you as hares with a sweet and sour sauce. It's an honor that you don't deserve, but generous people like me are more than willing to do a good deed."

He then walked over to Pinocchio and asked, "How did you manage to discover these thieves? To think that Melampo, my faithful Melampo, never found anything!"

The puppet might then have told him the whole story. He might have informed him of the disgraceful agreement that had been made between the dog and the weasels. But he remembered that the dog was dead, and he thought to himself, "What good is it to accuse the dead? The dead are dead, and the best thing to be done is to leave them in peace!"

"When the thieves got into the yard," the peasant continued, "were you asleep or awake?"

"I was asleep," answered Pinocchio, "but the weasels woke me with their chatter, and one of them came to the kennel and said, 'If you promise not to bark and wake the master, we'll make you a present of a fine, plucked chicken!' To think that they would have the audacity to make such a proposal to me! For although I am a puppet, possessing perhaps nearly all the faults in the world, there is one that I certainly will never be guilty of: dealing with, and sharing in the gains of, dishonest people!"

"Well said, my boy!" cried the peasant, slapping him on the shoulder. "Such sentiments do you honor, and as proof of my gratitude, I'll set you free at once. You may return home."

And he removed the dog collar.

{ Chapter 23 }

Pinocchio is left on his own

As soon as Pinocchio was released from the heavy and humiliating weight of the dog collar, he started off across the fields and did not stop until he had reached the high road that led to the fairy's house. When he reached it, he could see the woods where he had been so unfortunate as to meet with the fox and the cat. He could also see the top of the Big Oak from which he had hung. But although he looked in every direction, he could not see the little house belonging to the beautiful child with the blue hair.

Seized with a sad foreboding, he began to run as fast as he could, and in a few minutes he reached the field where the little white house had once stood. But the house was no longer there. He saw instead a marble stone, on which were engraved these sad words:

Here lies
the child with the blue hair
who died from sorrow
because she was abandoned by
her little brother Pinocchio

I leave you to imagine the puppet's feelings when he had with difficulty spelled out this epitaph. He fell to the ground, covered the tombstone with a thousand kisses, and then burst into an agony of tears. He cried all night, and when morning came, he was still crying, although he had no tears left. His sobs and lamentations were so heartbreaking that they echoed throughout the surrounding hills.

As he wept, he said, "Oh, little fairy, why did you die? Why didn't I die—I who

"Ah, yes, my boy," replied the pigeon, "when hunger is real, and there is nothing else to eat, even peas taste delicious. Hunger makes no distinction between good and bad food."

After quickly finishing their little meal, they flew away and continued their journey. The following morning, they reached the seashore.

The pigeon placed Pinocchio on the ground and, not wishing to be troubled with thanks for having done a good deed, flew quickly away and disappeared.

The shore was crowded with people who were looking out to sea, shouting and pointing.

"What has happened?" Pinocchio asked an old woman.

"A poor father who has lost his son has gone away in a boat to search for him on the other side of the sea. But today the water is so violent that the little boat is in danger of sinking!"

"Where is the little boat?"

"Out there, in line with my finger," said the old woman, pointing to a little boat that looked like a nutshell with a very little man in it.

Pinocchio fixed his eyes on it and then let out a piercing scream, crying, "It's my father! It's my father!"

The boat, beaten by the fury of the waves, disappeared for a moment in the trough of the sea, and then reappeared. Pinocchio, standing on top of a high rock, kept calling to his father by name, and making every kind of signal to him with his hands, his handkerchief, and his cap.

And although he was far off, Geppetto appeared to recognize his son, for he also took off his cap and waved it, and tried by gestures to make him understand that he would have returned if it had been possible, but the sea was so angry that he could not use his oars or approach the shore.

Suddenly, a tremendous wave rose, and the boat disappeared. The people waited, hoping the little boat would again come to the surface, but it was seen no more.

"Poor man!" said the fishermen who were assembled on the shore. They murmured a prayer and then turned to go home.

But just then they heard a desperate cry. Looking back, they saw a little boy jump from a rock into the sea, yelling, "I'll save my father!"

Pinocchio, being made of wood, floated easily, and he swam like a fish. One moment they saw him disappear under the water, carried down by the fury of the waves, and the next they could see an arm or a leg. At last they lost sight of him, and he was seen no more.

"Poor boy!" said the fishermen who were collected on the shore. They murmured a prayer and then returned home.

❧

{ *Chapter 24* }

The Island of the Busy Bees

oping to be in time to save his father, Pinocchio swam the whole night.

And what a horrible night it was! The rain came down in sheets. It hailed and thundered. And the flashes of lightning made it as light as day.

Towards morning he saw a long strip of land not far off. It was an island in the midst of the sea.

He tried his best to reach the shore, but it was all in vain. The waves knocked him about as if he was a stick or a wisp of straw. At last, fortunately for him, a wave rolled up with such fury that he was lifted up and thrown violently onto the sand.

He struck the ground with such force that his ribs and all his joints rattled, but he comforted himself by saying, "That was a wonderful escape!"

Little by little the sky cleared, the sun shone in all its splendor, and the sea became as quiet and smooth as oil.

The puppet spread his clothes to dry in the sun and began to look in every direction in hopes of seeing a little boat on the water with a little man in it. But although he looked and looked, he could see nothing but the sky, the sea, and the sail of a ship that looked no bigger than a fly.

"If I only knew what this island was called!" he said. "If I only knew whether it

was inhabited by civilized people—that is, by people who don't hang boys from the branches of trees. But whom can I ask if there is nobody?"

The idea of finding himself alone, all alone, in the midst of this uninhabited country made him so melancholy that he was about to cry. But at that moment, he saw a big fish swimming by, a short distance from the shore. It was going quietly about its own business, with its head out of the water.

Not knowing its name, the puppet called out in a loud voice, "Hello, Mr. Fish! May I have a word with you?"

"Two if you like," answered the fish, who was a dolphin, and so polite that few like him are to be found in any sea in the world.

"Would you be kind enough to tell me if there are villages on this island where I could find something to eat, without running the risk of being eaten?"

"Certainly there are," replied the dolphin. "You'll find one just a short distance from here."

"And what road must I take to get there?"

"Take the path to your left and follow your nose. You can't make a mistake."

"Would you tell me something else? Since you swim in the sea all day and all night, have you by chance met a little boat with my father in it?"

"And who is your father?"

"He is the best father in the world—and it would be difficult to find a worse son than I."

"During the terrible storm last night," answered the dolphin, "the little boat must have sunk."

"And my father?"

"He must have been swallowed by the terrible shark that has been spreading devastation and ruin in our waters for some time."

"Is this shark very big?" asked Pinocchio, who was already beginning to shake with fear.

"Big?" replied the dolphin. "To give you some idea, I'll tell you that he is bigger than a five-story house, and that his mouth is so enormous and so deep that a railway train with its smoking engine could easily pass down his throat."

"Mercy!" exclaimed the terrified puppet. Putting on his clothes with the greatest haste, he said to the dolphin, "Good-bye, Mr. Fish. I'm sorry for the trouble I've caused you. Many thanks for your politeness!"

He then took the path that had been pointed out to him and began to walk fast—so fast, in fact, that he was almost running. And at the slightest noise he turned to look behind him, fearing he might see the terrible shark with a railway train in its mouth chasing him.

After walking for half an hour, he reached a little village called The Village of the Busy Bees. The road was alive with people running here and there on business. All were at work. All had something to do. You could not have found an idler or a vagabond, not even if you had searched in every nook and cranny.

"Ah!" said that lazy Pinocchio at once, "I see that this village will never suit me! I wasn't born to work!"

By this time, however, he was tormented by hunger, for he had not eaten anything for twenty-four hours—not even a few peas. What was he to do?

There were only two ways by which he could obtain food—ask for work, or beg for a penny or a mouthful of bread.

He was ashamed to beg, for his father had always preached that no one had a right to beg except the aged and the weak. The really poor in this world, deserving

of compassion and assistance, are those who, from age or sickness, are no longer able to earn their own living with the labor of their hands. It is the duty of everyone else to work. And if they won't work, so much the worse for them if they suffer from hunger.

At that moment a man came down the road, tired and panting. He was dragging along—with fatigue and difficulty—two carts full of coal.

Pinocchio, judging by his face that he was a kind man, approached him, cast his eyes down with shame, and said in a low voice, "Would you give me a penny, for I'm dying of hunger!"

"Not a penny," said the man, "but I'll pay you two pennies if you help me drag these two carts of coal home."

"I'm surprised by you!" answered the puppet, quite offended. "Let me tell you that I'm not accustomed to doing the work of a donkey. I've never drawn a cart!"

"All right then," answered the man. "But, my boy, if you're really dying of hunger, eat two fine slices of your pride, and be careful not to get indigestion."

A few minutes later a mason passed down the road, carrying on his shoulders a basket of mortar.

"Good man, would you give a penny to a poor boy who is aching for food?"

"Willingly," answered the man. "Come with me and carry the mortar, and instead of a penny I'll give you five."

"But the mortar is heavy," objected Pinocchio, "and I don't want to tire myself."

"If you don't want to tire yourself, then, my boy, amuse yourself with your aching, and much good may it do you."

In less than half an hour, twenty other people went by, and Pinocchio asked charity of them all, but they all answered, "Aren't you ashamed to beg? Instead of idling about the roads, go and look for a little work and learn to earn your bread."

At last a kind little woman carrying two pitchers of water came by.

"Will you let me drink a little water out of one of your pitchers?" asked Pinocchio, who was burning with thirst.

"Drink, my boy, if you wish!" said the little woman, setting down the two pitchers.

Pinocchio drank like a fish, and as he dried his mouth he mumbled, "I've quenched my thirst. If I could only appease my hunger!"

Hearing these words, the good woman said, "If you'll help me carry these pitchers of water home, I'll give you a fine piece of bread."

Pinocchio looked at the pitcher and answered neither yes or no.

"And besides the bread you'll have a nice dish of cauliflower, dressed with oil and vinegar," added the good woman.

Pinocchio looked at the pitcher again and answered neither yes or no.

"And after the cauliflower I'll give you some sweets."

This last temptation was so great that Pinocchio could not resist any longer. "Yes," he said, "I'll carry the pitcher to your house."

The pitcher was heavy, and the puppet, not being strong enough to carry it in his hands, had to carry it on his head.

When they reached the house, the good little woman made Pinocchio sit down at a small table, and she placed before him the bread, the cauliflower, and the sweets.

Pinocchio did not eat—he devoured. His stomach was like a house that had been left empty and uninhabited for five months.

When his ravenous hunger was somewhat appeased, he raised his head to thank the little woman. But he had no sooner looked at her than he uttered a prolonged "Oh-h-h!" of astonishment. He stared at her with wide eyes, his fork in the air, and his mouth full of bread and cauliflower, as if he had been bewitched.

"What has surprised you so much?" asked the good woman, laughing.

"It's—" answered the puppet. "It's—it's that you are like—that you remind me—yes, yes, yes, the same voice—the same eyes, the same hair—yes, yes, yes—you also have blue hair, as she had! Oh, little fairy! Tell me that it's you! Don't make me cry any more! If only you knew! I've cried so much. I've suffered so much!"

Having said this, Pinocchio threw himself at her feet, embraced the knees of the mysterious little woman, and began to cry bitterly.

❧

{ Chapter 25 }

Pinocchio promises to be good and studious

 t first the good woman maintained that she was not the little fairy with blue hair, but seeing that she was discovered, and not wishing to continue the charade any longer, she made herself known and said to Pinocchio, "You little rascal! How did you know who I was?"

"It was my great affection for you that told me."

"Do you remember? You left me when I was a child, and now I'm a woman— a woman almost old enough to be your mother."

"I'm delighted by that, for now instead of calling you my sister, I'll call you Mother. I've always wanted to have a mother like other boys have! But how did you manage to grow so fast?"

"That's a secret."

"Tell me, for I would also like to grow."

"But you can't grow," replied the fairy.

"Why?"

"Because puppets never grow. They are born puppets, they live puppets, and they die puppets."

"Oh, I'm sick of being a puppet!" cried Pinocchio, giving himself a slap on the head. "It's time that I became a man!"

"And you will become one, if you deserve it."

"Really? And what can I do to deserve it?"

"A very easy thing: learn to be a good boy."

"And you think I'm not?"

"You are quite the contrary. Good boys are obedient, and you—"

"And I never obey."

"Good boys like to learn and to work, and you—"

"And I lead an idle, vagabond life year-round."

"Good boys always speak the truth—"

"And I always tell lies."

"Good boys go willingly to school—"

"And school gives me pain all over my body. But starting today, I'll change my ways."

"Do you promise?"

"I promise. I'll become a good boy, and I'll make my father proud. Where is my poor father?"

"I don't know."

"Will I ever see him again?"

"I think so. Yes, I am sure of it."

Hearing this answer, Pinocchio was so delighted that he took the fairy's hands and began to kiss them. Then, raising his face and looking at her lovingly, he asked, "Tell me, Mother, then it wasn't true that you were dead?"

"It seems not," said the fairy, smiling.

"If you only knew the sorrow I felt and the tightening of my throat when I read, 'Here lies—'"

"I know, and that's why I have forgiven you. I saw from the sincerity of your grief that you had a good heart; and when boys have good hearts, even if they are scamps and have bad habits, there's always hope. That is, there's always hope that they will turn to better ways. That's why I came to look for you. I will be your mother."

"Oh, how delightful!" shouted Pinocchio, jumping for joy.

"You must obey me and do everything that I ask of you."

"Oh yes, yes, yes!"

"Tomorrow," said the fairy, "you will start going to school."

Pinocchio became at once a little less joyful.

"Then you must choose a profession or trade to follow."

Pinocchio became quite somber.

"What are you muttering between your teeth?" asked the fairy sharply.

"I was saying," moaned the puppet, "that it seemed to me too late to go to school now."

"No, my boy. Remember, it's never too late to learn."

"But I don't want to learn a profession or a trade."

"Why?"

"Because it tires me to work."

"My boy," said the fairy, "those who talk that way almost always end up either in prison or the hospital. Let me tell you that every man, whether he is born rich or poor, is obliged to do something in this world—to occupy himself, to work. Woe to those who lead slothful lives. Sloth is a dreadful illness and must be cured at once, in childhood, for once we are old, it can never be cured."

Touched by these words, Pinocchio lifted his head quickly and said, "I'll study, I'll work, I'll do all that you tell me, for I have become weary of being a puppet, and I want to become a boy at any price. You promised me that I could, didn't you?"

"I did promise, and now it depends on you."

※

{ Chapter 26 }

Pinocchio goes to see the shark

he following day, Pinocchio went to school.

Imagine the delight of all the mischievous boys when they saw a puppet walk into their school! They laughed as though they would never stop. They played all sorts of jokes on him. One boy carried off his cap, and another pulled his jacket. One tried to draw an ink mustache under his nose, and another tried to tie strings to his hands and feet to make him dance.

At first, Pinocchio pretended not to care. But at last he lost all patience and, turning to those who were teasing and making fun of him the most, said, "Beware, boys. I didn't come here to be your buffoon. I respect others, and I expect to be respected."

"Well said, clown! You've spoken like a book!" howled the young rascals, convulsing with laughter. One of them, more impertinent than the others, stretched out his hand, intending to seize the puppet by the end of his nose.

But he was not fast enough, for Pinocchio kicked the boy's shins under the table.

"Oh, what hard feet!" roared the boy, rubbing the bruise the puppet had given him.

"And what elbows! They're even harder than his feet!" said another, who had received a blow to the stomach for his rude jokes.

But the kick and the blow won Pinocchio the respect of all the boys in the school and they all made friends with him.

Even the schoolmaster praised him, for he found Pinocchio attentive, studious, and intelligent—always the first to come to school, and the last to leave when school was over.

But he had one fault: he made too many friends, and among them were several mischievous rascals who did not like to study.

The schoolmaster warned him every day, and the good fairy never failed to repeat it. "Be careful, Pinocchio!" she said. "Those bad classmates of yours will make you lose all love of study sooner or later, and they may even bring upon you some great misfortune."

"There's no chance of that!" answered the puppet, shrugging his shoulders and touching his forehead as if as to say, "There's too much sense here!"

Now it happened that one fine day, as he was on his way to school, Pinocchio met several of his usual companions, who asked, "Have you heard the great news?"

"No."

"In the sea near here, a shark as big as a mountain has appeared."

"Really? Can it be the same shark that was there when my poor father was drowned?"

"We're going to the shore to see him. Do you want to come?"

"No, I'm going to school."

"Who cares about school? We can go to school tomorrow. Whether we have a lesson more or a lesson less, we will always remain the same dumb donkeys."

"But what will the schoolmaster say?"

"The schoolmaster may say what he likes. He's paid to grumble all day."

"And my mother?"

"Mothers know nothing," answered the bad little boys.

"I know what I'll do," said Pinocchio. "I have reasons for wanting to see the shark, but I'll go and see him when school is over."

"Poor donkey!" exclaimed one of the boys. "Do you think that a fish of that size will wait for you? As soon as he is tired of being here, he'll leave for another place, and then it'll be too late."

"How long does it take to get from here to the shore?" asked the puppet.

"We can be there and back in an hour."

"Then away!" shouted Pinocchio. "And he who runs fastest is the best!"

At this, the boys, with their books under their arms, rushed off across the fields, and Pinocchio, who was always in the lead, seemed to have wings on his feet.

From time to time he turned to taunt his companions, who were some distance behind. Seeing them covered in dust, panting for breath, with their tongues hanging out of their mouths, he laughed heartily. The unfortunate puppet had no idea what terrors and dreadful disasters were awaiting him.

{ *Chapter 27* }

Pinocchio gets in a free-for-all fight

hen he arrived at the shore, Pinocchio looked out to sea, but he saw no shark. The sea was as smooth as a mirror.

"Where's the shark?" he asked, turning to his companions.

"He must have gone to breakfast," said one of them, laughing.

"Or he's taking a little nap," added another, laughing louder yet.

From their absurd answers and silly laughter Pinocchio deduced that his companions had been making a fool of him, and he said angrily, "And now may I ask what fun you could find in tricking me with the story of the shark?"

"Oh, it was great fun!" answered the little rascals in chorus.

"And in what way?"

"In making you miss school, and persuading you to come with us. Aren't you ashamed of always being so punctual and so diligent with your school work? Aren't you ashamed of studying so hard?"

"What business is it of yours if I study hard?"

"It concerns us a great deal, because it makes us look bad in the eyes of the schoolmaster."

"Why?"

"Because boys who study make those who, like us, have no desire to learn seem worse by comparison. And we don't like it. We have our pride, too!"

"Then what must I do to please you?"

"You must follow our example and hate school, lessons, and the schoolmaster—our three greatest enemies."

"And if I wish to continue my studies?"

"In that case we'll have nothing more to do with you, and at the first opportunity, we'll make you pay for it."

"Really," said the puppet, shaking his head, "you make me want to laugh."

"Careful, Pinocchio!" shouted the biggest of the boys. "We'll have none of your superior airs. Don't come here to crow over us! For if you're not afraid of us, we're not afraid of you. Remember that you are one, and we are seven."

"Seven, like the seven deadly sins," said Pinocchio with a shout of laughter.

"Listen to him! He's insulted us all! He called us the seven deadly sins!"

"Pinocchio, say you're sorry, or it'll be the worse for you!"

"Cuckoo!" sang the puppet, putting his forefinger to the end of his nose scoffingly.

"Pinocchio, you'll regret it!"

"Cuckoo!"

"We'll beat you like a donkey!"

"Cuckoo!"

"You'll go home with a broken nose!"

"Cuckoo!"

"I'll give you a cuckoo!" said the most courageous of the boys. "Take this to begin with, and keep it for your supper tonight!"

And with that, he struck Pinocchio on the head with his fist.

But the puppet, as was to be expected, immediately returned the blow, and the fight began.

Pinocchio, although he was alone, defended himself like a hero. He used his feet, which were made of the hardest wood, so effectively that he kept his enemies at a respectful distance. Wherever the puppet's feet touched, they left a bruise that would not easily be forgotten.

The boys, becoming furious at not being able to get close to the puppet, turned to other weapons. Opening their book bags, they started throwing their books at him—dictionaries, spelling books, geography books, and other textbooks. But Pinocchio was quick and had sharp eyes, and he always managed to duck in time so that the books passed over his head and fell into the sea.

Imagine how surprised the fish were! Thinking that the books were something to eat, they arrived in shoals. But after tasting a page or two, they spat it out quickly and grimaced as if to say, "We're accustomed to something much better!"

The battle was growing quite fierce when, suddenly, a big crab came out of the water. He climbed slowly onto the shore and called out, in a hoarse voice that sounded like a trombone with a bad cold, "Stop that, you young rascals! These fights among boys always end badly. Some disaster is sure to happen!"

Poor crab! He might as well have preached to the wind. Even that young rascal Pinocchio turned around and said rudely, "Hold your tongue, you tiresome crab! You better suck some lozenges to cure that cold in your throat. Or better yet, go to bed!"

Just then, the boys, who had no more books of their own to throw, saw Pinocchio's book bag lying on the ground and took possession of it in less time than it takes to tell.

Among the books was one bound in strong cardboard. It was called *A Treatise on Arithmetic*. I leave it to you to imagine if it was big or not!

One of the boys seized the volume, aimed at Pinocchio's head, and threw it as hard as he could. But instead of hitting the puppet, the book struck one of his companions on the head, who turned as white as a sheet and cried, "Oh, Mother, help me! I'm dying!" as he fell onto the sand. Thinking he was dead, the terrified boys ran away as fast as their legs could carry them, and in a few minutes they were out of sight.

But Pinocchio remained. Although he was more dead than alive from grief and fright, he soaked his handkerchief in the sea and began to bathe the temples of his poor schoolmate, crying bitterly and calling him by name. "Eugene! My poor Eugene! Open your eyes and look at me! Why don't you answer? I didn't do it. It wasn't I that hurt you! Believe me, it wasn't! Open your eyes, Eugene. If you keep your eyes shut, I'll die, too. Oh! What will I do? How will I ever return home? How will I ever have the courage to go back to my mother? What will become of me? Where can I run away to? Oh! How much better it would have been, a thousand times better, if I had gone to school! Why did I listen to my companions? They have been my ruin. The schoolmaster said to me, and my mother repeated it often, 'Beware of bad companions!' But I'm stubborn. A willful fool. I let them talk, and then I always go my own way! And I have to suffer for it. Because of this, ever since I was born, I've never had a happy quarter of an hour. Oh! What will become of me?"

Pinocchio cried and sobbed, struck his head with his fists, and called poor Eugene by name. Suddenly, he heard the sound of approaching footsteps.

He turned and saw two policemen.

"What are you doing there on the ground?" they asked Pinocchio.

"I'm helping my schoolmate."

"Has he been hurt?"

"So it seems."

"Hurt indeed!" said one of the policemen, stooping down and examining Eugene closely. "This boy has been wounded on the temple. Who did it?"

"Not I," stammered the puppet breathlessly.

"If it wasn't you, then who was it?"

"Not I," repeated Pinocchio.

"And what was he wounded with?"

"With this book." And the puppet picked up *A Treatise on Arithmetic* and showed it to the policeman.

"And to whom does this book belong?"

"To me."

"That's enough. We need nothing more. Get up and come with us at once."

"But I—"

"Come along with us!"

"But I'm innocent."

"Come along with us!"

Before they left, the policemen called to some fishermen who were passing near the shore in their boat, and said to them, "We place this wounded boy in your care. Carry him to your house and look after him. Tomorrow we'll come and see him again."

They then turned to Pinocchio, placed him between them, and said in commanding voices, "Forward! And step lively, or it will be the worse for you!"

Without waiting for them to repeat it, the puppet set out along the road leading to the village. The poor little devil hardly knew where he was. He thought he must be dreaming, and what a dreadful dream it was! He was beside himself. His eyes saw double, his legs shook, his tongue stuck to the roof of his mouth, and he could not utter a word. And yet, in the midst of his confusion, his heart was pierced by a cruel thorn—the thought that he would have to pass under the windows of the good fairy's house between two policemen. He would rather have died.

They had just reached the village when a gust of wind blew Pinocchio's cap off his head and carried it some ten yards away.

"Will you permit me," said the puppet to the policemen, "to go and get my cap?"

"Go, then. But be quick about it."

The puppet went and picked up his cap, but instead of putting it on his head, he took it between his teeth and ran as fast as he could toward the seashore.

The policemen, thinking it would be difficult to catch him, sent a large mastiff after him, one that had won first prize in all the dog races. Pinocchio ran, but the dog ran faster. People came to their windows and crowded into the street, anxious to see the end of the desperate race. But their curiosity was not satisfied, for Pinocchio and the dog raised such clouds of dust that in a few minutes nothing could be seen.

{ Chapter 28 }

Pinocchio is in danger of being fried

here came a moment in this desperate race—a terrible moment—when Pinocchio thought all was lost, for Alidoro—that was the mastiff's name—ran so swiftly that he had nearly caught him.

The puppet could hear the panting of the dreadful beast close behind him—mere inches separated the two—and could even feel the dog's hot breath.

Fortunately, the shore was close, and the sea just a few steps farther.

As soon as he reached the shore, the puppet made a wonderful leap—a frog could have done no better—and plunged into the water.

Alidoro tried to stop, but he had built up such great momentum that he went into the sea, too. The poor dog could not swim, but he made great efforts to keep his nose above water by paddling with his paws. Unfortunately, the more he struggled, the farther he sank under the water.

When he rose to the surface again, his eyes rolled with terror, and he barked, "I'm drowning! I'm drowning!"

"Drown, then!" shouted Pinocchio from a distance, seeing himself safe from all danger.

"Help me, Pinocchio! Save my life!"

At that agonizing cry the puppet, who truly had a kind heart, was moved with compassion. Turning to the dog, he said, "If I save your life, will you promise not to bother me further, and not to run after me?"

"I promise! I promise! Be quick, for pity's sake, for if you delay another half-minute I'll be dead!"

Pinocchio hesitated, but then he remembered his father's saying that a good deed is never forgotten. So, he swam to Alidoro, took hold of his tail with both hands, and brought him safe and sound onto the dry sand.

The poor dog could not stand. He had drunk, against his will, so much salt water that he had swelled up like a balloon. The puppet, however, not wanting to trust him completely, thought it better to jump back into the water. When he was some distance from the shore, he called out to the dog, "Good-bye, Alidoro! A good journey to you! And give my best to all at home!"

"Good-bye, Pinocchio," answered the dog. "A thousand thanks for saving my life. You've done me a great service, and in this world what is given is returned. If an occasion arises, I won't forget it."

Pinocchio swam on, keeping near the shore. At last he thought he had reached a safe place. He spotted a kind of cave among the rocks from which a cloud of smoke was rising.

"There must be a fire in that cave," he said to himself. "So much the better. I'll dry and warm myself, and then? And then we'll see."

Having made this decision, he approached the rocks. But just as he was going to climb up, he felt something under the water that rose higher and higher and carried him high into the air. He tried to escape, but it was too late, for to his extreme surprise he found himself enclosed in a great net, together with a swarm of fish of every size and shape, who were flapping and struggling as if they had gone mad.

At that same moment, a fisherman came out of the cave. He was so ugly, so horribly ugly, that he looked like a sea monster. His head was covered with a thick bush of green grass, his skin was green, his eyes were green, and his long beard was green. He looked like an immense lizard standing on its hind legs.

When the fisherman had drawn his net out of the sea, he exclaimed with great satisfaction, "Thank Heaven! I'll have a splendid feast of fish today!"

"How lucky I am not to be a fish!" said Pinocchio to himself, regaining a little courage.

The net full of fish was carried into the cave, which was dark and smoky. In the middle of the cave a large frying pan full of oil sputtered, producing a smell so rank that it took one's breath away.

"Now we'll see what fish we have caught!" said the green fisherman, and putting into the net an enormous hand—a hand so large and misshapen that it looked like a baker's shovel—he pulled out a handful of mullet.

"These mullet will be good!" he said. After he smelled them, he threw them into a pan without water.

He repeated the same process many times. And as he drew out the fish, his mouth watered, and he said, chuckling to himself, "What good whiting! What exquisite sardines! These crabs will be excellent! What delicious little anchovies!"

The last to remain in the net was Pinocchio.

No sooner had the fisherman taken him out than he opened his big green eyes and cried, half-frightened, "What sort of fish is this? I don't remember eating fish of this kind before!"

He looked at the puppet again, examined him all over, and ended by saying, "I know! He must be a crawfish!"

Pinocchio, upset at being mistaken for a crawfish, said in an angry voice, "A crawfish indeed! You take me for a crawfish? What treatment! I'm a puppet."

"A puppet?" replied the fisherman. "To tell the truth, a puppet is quite a new fish for me. All the better! I will eat you with greater pleasure."

"Eat me? Don't you understand? I'm not a fish! Don't you hear that I talk and reason as you do?"

"That's quite true," said the fisherman, "and because I see that you are a fish that can speak and reason, I'll treat you with all the consideration you deserve."

"What kind of consideration?"

"In token of my friendship, I'll give you the choice of how you would like to be cooked. Would you like to be fried in the frying pan, or would you prefer to be stewed with tomato sauce?"

"To tell the truth," answered Pinocchio, "if I'm to choose, I'd prefer to be set free so that I may return home."

"You're joking! Do you think I would pass on the opportunity to taste such a rare fish? It's not every day, I assure you, that a puppet fish is caught in these waters. Leave it to me. I'll fry you in the frying pan with the other fish, and you'll be quite satisfied. It's always better to be fried with company."

With that, the unhappy Pinocchio began to cry and scream and beg for mercy, sobbing, "How much better it would have been if I had gone to school! I listened to my companions, and now I'm paying for it! Boo-hoo-hoo!"

He wriggled like an eel, making indescribable efforts to slip out of the clutches of the green fisherman. But it was useless. The fisherman took a long rope, bound Pinocchio's hands and feet as if he had been a sausage, and threw him into the pan with the other fish.

He then fetched a wooden bowl full of flour and began to flour them each in turn. And as soon as they were ready, he threw them into the frying pan.

The first to dance in the boiling oil were the poor whiting. The crabs followed, then the sardines, and then the anchovies. At last it was Pinocchio's turn. Seeing himself so near death—and such a horrible death—he trembled so violently that he had neither voice nor breath left to beg for mercy.

But the poor boy pleaded with his eyes! The green fisherman, however, without caring in the least, plunged him five or six times in the flour, coating him from head to foot until he looked like a puppet made of plaster.

He then took Pinocchio by the head, and . . .

{ *Chapter 29* }

Pinocchio returns to the fairy

ust as the fisherman was about to throw Pinocchio into the frying pan, a large dog entered the cave, lured there by the strong and savory odor of fried fish.

"Get out!" shouted the fisherman threateningly, holding the floured puppet in his hand.

But the poor dog, who was as hungry as a wolf, whined and wagged his tail as if to say, "Give me a mouthful of fish, and I'll leave you in peace."

"Get out, I tell you!" repeated the fisherman, and he stretched out his leg to give him a kick.

But the dog, who was really hungry, would not be tossed aside. He turned on the fisherman, growling and showing his terrible teeth.

Just then a feeble little voice was heard in the cave crying, "Save me, Alidoro! If you don't save me, I'll be fried!"

The dog recognized Pinocchio's voice, and to his extreme surprise he discovered that it came from the floured bundle in the fisherman's hand.

So what do you think he did? He leaped, seized the bundle in his mouth, and, holding it gently between his teeth, rushed out of the cave like a flash of lightning.

The fisherman, furious at seeing a fish he was so eager to eat snatched from him, ran after the dog, but he had run only a few steps when he suffered a fit of coughing and had to give up the chase.

When he reached the path that led to the village, Alidoro stopped and put Pinocchio gently on the ground.

"How much I have to thank you for!" said the puppet.

"There's no need," replied the dog. "You saved me, and I've now saved you. You know that we must all help each other in this world."

"But what brought you to the cave?"

"I was lying on the shore more dead than alive, when the wind brought to me the smell of fried fish. The smell excited my appetite, and I followed it. If I had arrived a second later—"

"Don't speak of it!" groaned Pinocchio, who was still trembling with fright. "Don't speak of it! If you had arrived a second later, I would by this time have been fried, eaten, and digested. Brrr! It makes me shudder just to think of it!"

Alidoro, laughing, extended his right paw to the puppet, who shook it heartily as a sign of friendship, and then they parted.

The dog took the road home, and Pinocchio, left alone, went to a cottage not far off and said to a little old man who was warming himself in the sun, "Tell me, good man, do you know anything of a poor boy named Eugene who was wounded in the head?"

"The boy was brought by some fishermen to this cottage, and now—"

"And now he's dead!" interrupted Pinocchio with great sorrow.

"No, he's alive, and has returned to his home."

"Really? Really?" cried the puppet, dancing with delight. "Then the wound was not serious?"

"It might have been very serious, even fatal," answered the little old man, "for they threw a thick book bound in cardboard at his head."

"And who threw it at him?"

"One of his schoolmates, one named Pinocchio."

"And who is this Pinocchio?" asked the puppet, pretending ignorance.

"They say that he's a bad boy, a vagabond, a regular good-for-nothing."

"Lies! All lies!"

"Do you know this Pinocchio?"

"By sight!" answered the puppet.

"And what's your opinion of him?" asked the little man.

"He seems to me to be a very good boy, anxious to learn, and obedient and affectionate to his father and family."

While the puppet was firing off all these lies, he touched his nose and discovered that it had grown a few inches longer. Very much alarmed, he cried out, "Don't believe, good man, what I've been telling you! I know Pinocchio very well, and I can assure you that he is really a very bad boy, disobedient and idle, who instead of going to school runs off with his companions to amuse himself!"

As soon as he had spoken these words, his nose shrank back to its original size.

"And why are you so white?" asked the old man suddenly.

"I'll tell you. Without watching where I was going, I rubbed up against a wall that had just been whitewashed," answered the puppet, ashamed to confess that he had been floured like a fish prepared for the frying pan.

"And what have you done with your jacket, your trousers, and your cap?"

"I met with robbers who took them from me. Tell me, good man, could you perhaps give me some clothes to return home in?"

"My boy, I have nothing but a little sack in which I keep beans. If you want it, take it. You are welcome to it."

Pinocchio did not wait to be told twice. He took the sack, cut a hole in the end and one in each side, and put it on like a shirt. And in this crudely fashioned garb he set off for the village.

But as he went, he began to feel very uncomfortable; for each step forward, he took another step backward, saying to himself, "How will I ever face my good little fairy? What will she say when she sees me? Will she forgive me a second time? I'm afraid that she won't! Oh, I'm sure that she won't! And it serves me right, for I'm a rascal. I'm always promising

to better myself, and I never keep my word!"

It was night when Pinocchio reached the village. As a storm had come up, and it was raining very hard, he went straight to the fairy's house.

When he arrived, his courage failed him, and instead of knocking he ran away some twenty paces. He returned to the door a second time but could not make up his mind. He came back a third time, and still he dared not knock. The fourth time he took hold of the knocker and, trembling, gave a little knock.

He waited and waited. At last, after half an hour had passed, a window on the top floor opened—the house was four stories high—and Pinocchio saw a big snail with a lighted candle on her head looking out. She called to him, "Who's there at this hour?"

"Is the fairy home?" asked the puppet.

"The fairy is asleep and must not be awakened. But who are you?"

"It's I!"

"Who is I?"

"Pinocchio."

"And who is Pinocchio?"

"The puppet who lives in the fairy's house."

"Ah, I understand!" said the snail. "Wait for me there. I'll come down and open the door for you."

"Be quick, for pity's sake, for I'm dying of cold."

"My boy, I am a snail, and snails are never in a hurry."

An hour passed, and then two, and the door was still not opened. Pinocchio, who was soaked through and trembling from cold and fear, at last took courage and knocked again, and this time he knocked louder.

At this second knock, a window on the third floor opened, and the same snail appeared.

"Beautiful little snail," cried Pinocchio from the street, "I've been waiting for two hours! And two hours on such a bad night seem longer than two years. Be quick, for pity's sake!"

"My boy," answered the calm little snail, "I'm a snail, and snails are never in a hurry."

And the window was closed again.

Soon midnight struck, then one o'clock, then two o'clock, and still the door remained closed.

At last Pinocchio lost all patience and seized the knocker in a rage, intending to give a blow that would resound throughout the house. But the knocker, which was iron, suddenly turned into an eel, slipped out of his hands, and disappeared into the stream of water that ran down the middle of the street.

"Oh-ho!" shouted Pinocchio, blind with rage. "Since the knocker has disappeared, I'll kick instead with all my might!"

And drawing back his foot, he gave the house door a tremendous kick. The blow was so violent that his foot went through the wood and became stuck; when he tried to draw it back again, he couldn't, for it remained fixed like a nail that has been hammered down.

Think of poor Pinocchio! He had to spend the rest of the night with one foot on the ground and the other in the air.

Finally, at dawn, the door was opened. The little snail had rushed to the door, taking only nine hours to come down from the fourth floor.

"What are you doing with your foot stuck in the door?" she asked the puppet, laughing.

"It was an accident. Do try, beautiful little snail, to free me from this torture."

"My boy, that's the work of a carpenter, and I have never been a carpenter."

"Beg the fairy for me!"

"The fairy is asleep and must not be wakened."

"But what am I supposed to do all day, stuck in this door?"

"You can amuse yourself by counting the ants that pass down the street."

"At least bring me something to eat, for I'm terribly hungry."

"At once!" said the snail.

After three and a half hours, she returned to Pinocchio carrying a silver tray on her head. The tray held a loaf of bread, a roast chicken, and four ripe apricots.

"Here is the breakfast that the fairy has sent you," said the snail.

The puppet felt very comforted at the sight of these good things. But when he began to eat them, he was disgusted to find that the bread was made of plaster, the chicken cardboard, and the four apricots painted stone!

He wanted to cry. In his despair, he tried to throw away the tray and all that was on it; but instead, either from grief or exhaustion, he fainted.

When he came to, he found that he was lying on a sofa, with the fairy beside him.

"I'll forgive you once more," the fairy said. "But woe to you if you behave badly a third time!"

Pinocchio promised, and he swore that he would study, and that in the future he would always conduct himself well.

Pinocchio kept his word for the remainder of the year. Indeed, he became the best student in his school, and his behavior in general was so praiseworthy that the fairy was very pleased. One day she said to him, "Tomorrow your wish will be granted."

"Do you mean...?"

"Tomorrow you'll cease to be a wooden puppet, and you'll become a real boy."

No one who had not witnessed it could ever imagine Pinocchio's joy at hearing this long-awaited news. All his schoolmates were to be invited to a grand breakfast at the fairy's house the following day so that they might celebrate the great event together. The fairy had prepared two hundred cups of coffee and milk, and four hundred bread rolls buttered on both sides. The day promised to be most happy and delightful, but—

Unfortunately, in the lives of puppets, there is always a "but" that spoils everything.

{ *Chapter 30* }

Why there was no party

inocchio asked the fairy's permission to go around town and invite his friends to the party. The fairy said to him, "Yes, you may, but remember to return home before dark. Do you understand?"

"I promise to be back in an hour," answered the puppet.

"Be careful, Pinocchio! Children are always quick to make promises, but they are not so ready to keep them."

"But I'm not like other children. When I say something, I do it."

"We'll see. If you are disobedient again, so much the worse for you."

"Why?"

"Because children who don't listen to the advice of those who know more than they do always meet with some misfortune or other."

"I've learned my lesson," said Pinocchio. "I'll never make that mistake again."

"We'll see if that is true."

Without saying a word more, the puppet took leave of his good fairy, who was like a mother to him, and went out of the house singing and dancing.

In less than an hour, all his friends were invited. Some accepted at once. Others

hesitated at first, but when they heard that the rolls would be buttered on both sides, they said, "We'll be sure to be there!"

Now I must tell you that among Pinocchio's friends and schoolmates there was one that he liked best. This boy's name was Romeo, but he went by the nickname of Lampwick, because he was thin, straight, and bright—just like the new wick of a lamp.

Lampwick was the laziest, naughtiest boy in the school, but Pinocchio liked him just the same. In fact, he had gone to his house first to invite him to breakfast, but Lampwick was not there. The puppet returned a second time, but he was still away. He went a third time, but it was in vain. Where was he? Pinocchio looked here, there, and everywhere, and at last he saw him hiding in the porch of a peasant's cottage.

"What are you doing there?" asked Pinocchio.

"I'm waiting for midnight, so I can leave."

"Why, where are you going?"

"Very, very far away."

"I've been to your house three times looking for you."

"What did you want with me?"

"Don't you know about the great event? Haven't you heard of my good fortune?"

"What is it?"

"Tomorrow I cease to be a puppet, and I become a boy like you—like all the other boys."

"Much good may it do you!"

"Tomorrow, therefore, I expect you to have breakfast at my house."

"But I told you that I'm going away tonight."

"At what time?"

"In a short time."

"And where are you going?"

"I'm going to live in a faraway country—the most delightful country in the world. A real paradise!"

"What is it called?"

"It's called Playland. Why don't you come, too?"

"I? No, never!"

"You're wrong, Pinocchio. Believe me, if you don't come you'll be sorry. Where else could you find a better country for us boys? There are no schools, no schoolmasters, and no books. In that delightful land nobody ever studies. There's never school on Saturday, and every week consists of six Saturdays and one Sunday. Just think! Vacation starts on the first day of January and ends on the last day of December. That's the country for me! That's what all civilized countries should be like!"

"But how are the days spent in Playland?"

"They are spent in play and amusement from morning 'til night. When night comes, you go to bed, and in the morning, you start all over. What do you think of that?"

"Hmm!" said Pinocchio, shaking his head slightly as if to say, "That sort of life wouldn't be too bad!"

"Well, will you come with me? Yes or no? Make up your mind!"

"No. I promised my good fairy that I would become a good boy, and I'll keep my word. And as I see that the sun is setting, I must leave you at once. Good-bye, and a pleasant journey to you."

"Where are you rushing off to in such a hurry?"

"Home. My good fairy wants me to be back before dark."

"Wait another two minutes."

"I'll be late."

"Only two minutes."

"And if the fairy scolds me?"

"Let her scold. Once she has scolded, she will stop," said that rascal Lampwick.

"And how are you going? Alone or with companions?"

"Alone? There will be more than a hundred boys with me."

"Will you be making the journey on foot?"

"A stagecoach will pass by shortly to take me to that happy country."

"What I would not give for the stagecoach to pass by now!"

"Why?"

"That I might see you all off together."

"Stay a little while longer, and you can do so."

"No, no, I must go home."

"Wait another two minutes."

"I've already delayed too long. The fairy will be worried about me."

"Poor fairy! Is she afraid that the bats will eat you?"

"But are you really certain that there are no schools in that country?" Pinocchio asked.

"Not a single one."

"And no schoolmasters either?"

"Not one."

"And no one ever has to study?"

"Never, never, never!"

"What a delightful country!" said Pinocchio. "I've never been there, but I can quite imagine it."

"Why don't you come, too?"

"It's useless to tempt me. I promised my good fairy that I would become a sensible boy, and I won't break my word."

"Good-bye, then, and give my best to all the other boys at school, if you meet them in the street."

"Good-bye, Lampwick: a pleasant journey to you! Have a wonderful time, and think of your friends now and then."

Upon saying this, the puppet made two steps to go, but then he stopped, turned to his friend, and asked, "But are you quite certain that in that country all the weeks consist of six Saturdays and one Sunday?"

"Most certain."

"Do you know for sure that vacation begins on the first day of January and ends on the last day of December?"

"Quite sure."

"What a delightful country!" repeated Pinocchio, looking enchanted. Then, with a resolute air, he added, "Good-bye for the last time, and a pleasant journey to you. When do you leave?"

"A little more than an hour from now."

"What a pity! If it were only one hour, I would almost be tempted to wait."

"And the fairy?"

"It's already late. If I return home an hour later, it will be all the same."

"Poor Pinocchio! And if the fairy scolds you?"

"I'll let her scold. Once she has scolded well, she'll stop."

In the meantime, it had become quite dark. Suddenly they saw a small light moving in the distance. They heard people talking and the sound of a trumpet, small and feeble like the hum of a mosquito.

"Here it is!" shouted Lampwick, jumping to his feet.

"What is it?" asked Pinocchio in a whisper.

"It's the stagecoach coming for me. Will you come, too? Yes or no?"

"But is it really true," asked the puppet, "that in that country children never have to study?"

"Never, never, never!"

"What a delightful country! What a marvelous country!"

{ Chapter 31 }

The puppet sets out for Playland

At last the stagecoach arrived, and it did so without making the slightest noise, for its wheels were bound with rags.

It was drawn by twelve pairs of donkeys, all the same size, but of different colors. Some were gray, some were white, and some were spotted like pepper and salt. Others had large stripes of yellow and blue.

But the most extraordinary thing was that the twelve pairs—that is, the twenty-four donkeys—were not shod like other beasts of burden. Instead, they had on their feet men's boots made of white leather.

And the coachman?

Picture a little man broader than he is tall, soft and greasy like a lump of butter, with a round face like an orange, a little mouth that is always laughing, and a soft, caressing voice like that of a cat when it is meowing to the mistress of the house for some cream.

All the boys liked him as soon as they saw him, and they hurried to find a place in his coach, eager to be taken to the true land of paradise known on the map as Playland.

The coach was quite full of boys between eight and twelve years old, heaped one atop the other like herrings in a barrel. They were uncomfortable, packed close together,

and could hardly breathe. But nobody said "Ow!" Nobody grumbled. The consolation of knowing that in a few hours they would reach a country where there were no books, no schools, and no schoolmasters made them so happy that they felt neither fatigue nor discomfort, neither hunger, nor thirst, nor lack of sleep.

As soon as the stagecoach stopped, the little man turned to Lampwick and, with a thousand smirks and grimaces, said to him, "Tell me, my fine boy, would you like to go to that happy country?"

"I certainly would!"

"But I must tell you, my dear child, that there is not a place left in the coach. You can see for yourself that it's quite full."

"No matter," replied Lampwick. "If there is no place inside, I'll manage to sit outside on the crossbar." And with a leap he seated himself astride the crossbar.

"And you, my love!" said the little man, turning in a flattering manner to Pinocchio. "What do you intend to do? Are you coming with us, or are you going to remain behind?"

"I'm going to remain behind," answered Pinocchio. "I'm going home. I intend to study and go to school, as all good children do."

"Much good may it do you!"

"Pinocchio," cried Lampwick, "listen to me. Come with us, and we'll have such fun."

"No, no, no!"

"Come with us, and we'll have such fun!" cried four other voices from inside the coach.

"Come with us, and we'll have such fun!" shouted a hundred voices in chorus from inside the coach.

"But if I come with you, what will my good fairy say?" said the puppet, who was beginning to give in to the pressure.

"Don't worry about that," said Lampwick. "Think only that we are going to a country where we'll be free to play from morning 'til night."

Pinocchio did not answer. He only sighed. Then he sighed again. Finally, after sighing a third time, he said, "Make a little room for me! I'm coming too!"

"The places are all full," replied the little man. "But to show you how happy I am that you're with us, you may have my seat on the box."

"And you?"

"Oh, I'll go on foot."

"No, I couldn't allow that. I would rather mount one of these donkeys," cried Pinocchio.

Upon saying this, he approached the right-hand donkey of the first pair and attempted to mount it. But the animal turned and kicked him in the stomach, sending him sprawling with his legs in the air.

You can imagine the laughter of all the boys who witnessed this scene.

But the little man did not laugh. He approached the rebellious donkey and, pretending to give it a kiss, bit off half its ear.

Pinocchio, in the meantime, had gotten up from the ground in a fury, and with a leap he seated himself on the poor animal's back. He leaped so splendidly that the boys stopped laughing and began to shout, "Hurrah, Pinocchio!" They clapped their hands and applauded as if they would never stop.

But the donkey suddenly kicked up its hind legs and threw the poor puppet into the middle of the road.

The roars of laughter started again, but the little man, instead of laughing, felt such affection for the unruly donkey that he kissed it again, and in doing so bit half of its other ear off. He then said to the puppet, "Mount him now without fear. That little donkey is very stubborn, but I whispered something into its ears which has, I hope, made him gentle and reasonable."

Pinocchio mounted, and the stagecoach started to move. While the donkeys were galloping and the coach was rattling over the stones of the road, the puppet thought he heard a low voice that could barely be heard saying to him, "Poor fool! You've decided to do as you please, but you'll be sorry for it!"

Pinocchio was frightened and looked from side to side to discover where these words had come from, but he saw nobody. The donkeys galloped, the stagecoach rattled, the boys inside slept, Lampwick snored, and the little man seated on the box sang between his teeth:

> *"Everybody sleeps through the night,*
> *But I never sleep. . . ."*

After they had gone another mile, Pinocchio heard the same low voice saying to him, "Bear it in mind, you fool! Children who refuse to study, and turn their backs on books, schools, and schoolmasters, to pass their time in play and amusement, sooner or later come to a bad end. I know this from experience, and I can tell you. A day will come when you'll weep as I am weeping now, but then it will be too late!"

Upon hearing these words whispered very softly, the puppet, more frightened than ever, sprang down from the back of his donkey and went and took hold of its bridle.

Imagine his surprise when he saw that the donkey was crying, just like a boy!

"Excuse me, Mr. Coachman," cried Pinocchio to the little man. "I've discovered an extraordinary thing! This donkey is crying."

"Let it cry. It will laugh when it gets some hay."

"Have you taught it to talk?"

"No, but it spent three years in the company of trained dogs, and it learned to mutter a few words."

"Poor beast!"

"Come, come," said the little man, "let's not waste time watching a donkey cry. Mount him, and let's go on. The night is cold, and the road is long."

Pinocchio obeyed without another word. In the morning, about daybreak, they arrived safely in Playland.

It was a country unlike any other country in the world. The population was composed entirely of children. The oldest were fourteen, and the youngest barely eight

years old. In the streets there was such merriment, noise, and shouting, that it was enough to make a person's head spin. There were children everywhere. Some were playing with nuts, some with shuttlecocks, and some with balls. Some rode bicycles, while others rode wooden horses. A group was playing hide and seek, and a few children were chasing each other. Some children were acting, some singing, some turning somersaults. Some were amusing themselves by walking on their hands, with their feet in the air. Others were spinning hoops, or strutting about dressed as generals, wearing leaf helmets and commanding a squadron of cardboard soldiers. Some were laughing, and some were shouting. Others clapped their hands, or whistled, or clucked like hens who had just laid an egg. In short, it was such an uproar that—without cotton balls in both ears—a person might have gone deaf. Here and there, canvas theaters had been erected, and they were crowded with children from morning 'til night. Inscriptions were written in charcoal on the walls of the houses: "Long live toys!" "No more schools!" "Down with arithmetic!" and other fine sentiments, all misspelled.

Pinocchio, Lampwick, and the other boys who had made the journey with the little man had barely set foot in the town before they became part of the crowd, making friends with everybody in just a few minutes. Where could happier or more contented children be found?

In the midst of continual games and every sort of amusement, the hours, days, and weeks passed like lightning.

"Oh, what a delightful life!" said Pinocchio whenever he met Lampwick.

"See, then, wasn't I right?" replied Lampwick. "And to think that you didn't want to come! To think that you had intended to return home to your fairy, and to waste your time studying! If you are free today from the bother of books and school, you must admit that you owe it to me and my advice. Only a real friend would show such great kindness."

"It's true, Lampwick! If I'm now a happy boy, it is all your doing. And do you know what the schoolmaster used to say when he spoke of you? He always said to me, 'Don't have anything to do with that rascal Lampwick, for he's a bad companion and will lead you into mischief!'"

"Poor schoolmaster!" replied the other, shaking his head. "I know only too well that he disliked me and amused himself by speaking ill of me. But I'm generous, and I forgive him!"

"Noble soul!" said Pinocchio, embracing his friend and kissing him on the forehead.

This delightful life went on for five months, without a thought for books or school, when one morning, Pinocchio awoke to a most unpleasant surprise that put him in very bad spirits.

{ Chapter 32 }

Pinocchio turns into a donkey, tail and all

hat was this surprise?

I'll tell you, my dear readers. The surprise was that Pinocchio, when he awoke, scratched his head. And while scratching his head he discovered—can you guess what he discovered?

He discovered, to his great astonishment, that his ears had grown several inches!

You must know that the puppet had always had very small ears—so small that they were not visible to the naked eye. So you can imagine how he felt when he found that his ears had become so long during the night that they seemed like two brooms.

He went at once in search of a mirror so that he could look at himself. Not being able to find one, he filled his wash bowl with water, looked into it, and saw reflected what he certainly would never have wished to see. He saw his head adorned with a magnificent pair of donkey's ears!

Just think of poor Pinocchio's sorrow, shame, and despair!

He began to cry and howl, and he beat his head against the wall. But the more he cried, the longer his ears grew. They grew and grew and became hairy at the tips.

At the sound of his loud cries, a beautiful little squirrel that lived on the first floor came into the room. Seeing the puppet in such grief, she asked, "What's the matter, my dear neighbor?"

"I'm ill, my dear little squirrel, very ill—and with an illness that frightens me. Do you know how to take a pulse?"

"I think so."

"Then feel, and see if I have a fever."

The little squirrel raised her right forepaw, felt Pinocchio's pulse, and then said with a sigh, "My friend, I'm sorry to give you bad news!"

"What is it?"

"You have a very bad fever!"

"What kind of fever is it?"

"Donkey fever."

"That's a fever I don't understand," said the puppet, but he understood only too well.

"Then I'll explain it to you," said the squirrel, "for you must know that in two or three hours you will no longer be a puppet, or a boy."

"Then what will I be?"

"In two or three hours you will become a little donkey, like those that draw carts and carry cabbages and salad to market."

"Oh! Poor me! Poor me!" cried Pinocchio, seizing his ears with his hands and pulling them furiously as if they belonged to somebody else.

"My dear boy," said the squirrel, trying to console him, "what can you do to prevent it? It is destiny. It is written in the decrees of wisdom that all children who are lazy; who take a dislike to books, schools, and schoolmasters; and who pass their time in amusement and games must end up becoming little donkeys sooner or later."

"Is that really true?" asked the puppet, sobbing.

"It's only too true I'm afraid! And tears are now useless. You should have thought of that sooner!"

"But it wasn't my fault! Believe me, little squirrel, the fault was all Lampwick's!"

"And who is this Lampwick?"

"One of my schoolmates. I wanted to go home! I wanted to be obedient! I wanted to study and be a good boy! But Lampwick said to me, 'Why should you bother yourself with studying? Why should you go to school? Come with us instead to Playland, for there we won't have to learn. We'll amuse ourselves from morning to night, and we'll always be merry.'"

"And why did you follow the advice of that false friend—of that bad companion?"

"Why? Because, my dear little squirrel, I'm a puppet with no sense—and with no heart. Oh, if I only had the least heart, I would never have left that good fairy who loved me like a mother and did so much for me! And I would no longer be a puppet, for I would by this time have become a boy! But if I meet Lampwick, woe to him! He'll hear what I think of him!"

And he turned to leave. But when he reached the door, he remembered his donkey's ears, and feeling ashamed to show them in public, what do you think he did? He took a big cotton cap, put it on his head, and pulled it down to his nose.

He then set out, searching everywhere for Lampwick. He looked for him in the streets, in the squares, in the little theaters, in every possible place, but he could not find him. He asked everybody he met, but no one had seen him.

At last he went to his house and knocked on the door.

"Who is it?" asked Lampwick from within.

"Pinocchio!" answered the puppet.

"Wait a moment, and I'll let you in."

After half an hour the door was opened, and imagine Pinocchio's feelings when he saw his friend Lampwick with a big cotton cap on his head pulled down to his nose.

At the sight of the cap, Pinocchio felt almost comforted, and thought to himself, "Does my friend have the same illness I have? Is he also suffering from donkey fever?"

Pretending to have noticed nothing, he smiled and asked, "How are you, my dear Lampwick?"

"Very well. As well as a mouse in a block of cheese."

"Do you mean that?"

"Why should I tell you a lie?"

"Excuse me, but why, then, do you wear that cotton cap pulled over your ears?"

"The doctor ordered me to wear it because I've hurt my knee. And you, dear puppet, why are you wearing that cotton cap pulled down to your nose?"

"The doctor ordered me to wear it because I've hurt my foot."

"Oh, poor Pinocchio!"

"Oh, poor Lampwick!"

A long silence followed, during which the two friends did nothing but look knowingly at each other.

At last the puppet said softly, "Satisfy my curiosity, my dear Lampwick. Have you ever suffered from a disease of the ears?"

"Never! And you?"

"Never! Except that one of my ears was aching this morning."

"Mine, too."

"Yours, too? And which of your ears hurts?"

"Both of them. And you?"

"Both of them. Do you think we have the same illness?"

"I fear so."

"Will you do me a favor, Lampwick?"

"Yes, with all my heart."

"Will you let me see your ears?"

"Why not? But first, my dear Pinocchio, I'd like to see yours."

"No, you must be the first."

"No, my friend. First you, and then I!"

"Well," said the puppet, "let's agree like good friends."

"What to?"

"We'll take off our caps at the same time. Agreed?"

"Agreed."

And Pinocchio began to count in a loud voice, "One! Two! Three!"

At the word "three," they took off their caps and threw them into the air.

And then a scene followed that would seem incredible if it was not true. When Pinocchio and Lampwick discovered that they were both struck with the same misfortune, instead of feeling full of grief or shame, they tried to wag their ears and made fun of each other until they burst into laughter.

They laughed, and laughed, and laughed. But in the midst of their merriment, Lampwick suddenly stopped. He staggered, turned pale, and said to his friend, "Help, help, Pinocchio!"

"What's the matter?"

"Alas, I can no longer stand upright!"

"Neither can I!" exclaimed Pinocchio, tottering and beginning to cry.

And while they were talking, they doubled over and began to run around the room on their hands and feet. As they ran, their hands became hoofs, their faces lengthened into muzzles, and their backs became covered with a gray, hairy coat sprinkled with black.

But do you know what the worst moment for these two wretched boys was? The worst, most humiliating moment was when they felt their tails growing. Overcome with shame and sorrow, they began to weep and lament their fate.

Oh, if only they had kept quiet! For instead of sighs and lamentations, they could only bray like donkeys, and they brayed loudly in unison: "Hee-haw! Hee-haw!"

At this moment somebody knocked on the door, and a voice on the outside said, "Open the door! I'm the little man, the coachman who brought you to this country. Open at once, or it will be the worse for you!"

⚜

{ Chapter 33 }

Pinocchio becomes a trick donkey

hen they did not open the door, the little man forced it open with a violent kick. Coming into the room, he said to Pinocchio and Lampwick, "Well done, boys! You brayed well, and I recognized you by your voices. That's why I am here."

The two little donkeys became silent and stood with their heads down, their ears lowered, and their tails between their legs.

At first the little man stroked and patted them. Then, taking out a currycomb, he combed them 'til they shone like two mirrors. He put halters around their necks and led them to the marketplace in hopes of selling them and making a good profit.

The little man found plenty of buyers. Lampwick was bought by a peasant whose donkey had died the previous day. Pinocchio was sold to the director of a company of clowns and tightrope walkers, who intended to teach him to leap and dance with the other animals in the company.

And now, my little readers, do you see the fine trade that the little man pursued? The wicked little monster, who had a face that seemed sweet and innocent, made frequent journeys around the world with his stagecoach. As he went along, he collected, with promises and flattery, all the idle children who had taken a dislike to books and school. As soon as his coach was full, he took them to Playland so that they might pass their time playing games. And when, from continual play and no study, these poor, deluded children had become little donkeys, the man happily carried them off to fairs and markets to be sold. In this way, he made heaps of money in just a few years and became rich.

What became of Lampwick, I don't know, but Pinocchio, from the very first day, endured a very hard life.

When he was put into his stall, his master filled the manger with straw, but Pinocchio, having tried a mouthful, spat it out.

Then his master, grumbling, filled the manger with hay, but Pinocchio didn't like the hay either.

"So!" exclaimed his master. "Hay does not please you either? Leave it to me, my fussy donkey. I'll find a way to cure you!"

With that, he struck Pinocchio's legs with a whip.

Pinocchio began to cry and brayed, "Hee-haw! I can't digest straw!"

"Then eat hay!" said his master, who understood donkey dialect perfectly.

"Hee-haw! Hay gives me a pain in my stomach."

"Do you mean to tell me that a little donkey like you must be fed chicken breasts and other fine foods?" asked the master, getting more and more angry, and whipping him again.

At this second whipping, Pinocchio wisely held his tongue and said nothing more.

The stable was then shut, and Pinocchio was left alone. He had not eaten for many hours, and he began to yawn from hunger. When he yawned, his mouth seemed as wide as an oven.

At last, finding nothing else in the manger, he resigned himself to chewing a little hay. After he chewed it well, he shut his eyes and swallowed it.

"This hay is not bad," he said to himself, "but how much better it would have been if I had gone on with my studies! Instead of hay I might now be eating a loaf of fresh bread and a fine slice of sausage. But I must have patience!"

When he woke up the next morning, he looked in the manger for a little more hay, but he found none, for he had eaten all night long.

So he took a mouthful of chopped straw. But while he was chewing it, he could not help thinking that the taste of chopped straw did not in the least resemble a savory dish of macaroni or rice.

"But I must have patience!" he repeated as he went on chewing. "Perhaps my example will at least serve as a warning to all disobedient children who don't want to study. Patience! Patience!"

"Patience indeed!" shouted his master, coming into the stable. "Do you think, my little donkey, that I bought you only to give you food and drink? I bought you to make you work so that you might earn money for me. Up, then, at once! You must come with me into the ring, and there I'll teach you to jump through hoops, to break through paper frames with your head, to dance waltzes and polkas, and to stand upright on your hind legs."

One way or another, poor Pinocchio had to learn all these fine tricks. But it was three months before he had learned them, and he received many a whipping that nearly took his skin off.

At last the day came when his master was able to announce an extraordinary performance. Posters were stuck on the street corners heralding the event.

On that evening, as you may imagine, the theater was full an hour before the performance was to begin.

There was not a place to be had either in the pit, the stalls, or the boxes—not even for its weight in gold.

The benches around the ring were crowded with children who were in a fever of curiosity to see the famous little donkey Pinocchio dance.

When the first part of the performance

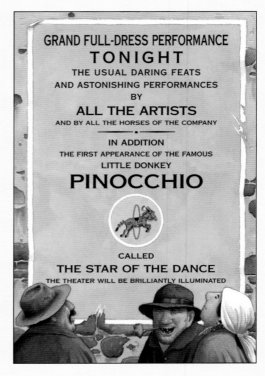

was over, the ringmaster, dressed in a black coat, white shorts, and big leather boots that came above his knees, introduced himself to the audience. Making a deep bow, he recited the following ridiculous speech: "Respectable public, ladies and gentlemen! The humble undersigned, being a passerby in this illustrious city, wishes to have the honor, not to say the pleasure, of presenting to this intelligent and distinguished audience a celebrated little donkey, who has already had the honor of dancing in the presence of the crowned heads of Europe.

"And thanking you for your attention, I beg of you to help us with your inspiring presence and to forgive us our shortcomings."

This speech was received with much laughter and applause. But the applause redoubled and became tumultuous when the little donkey Pinocchio made his appearance in the middle of the ring. He was decked out for the occasion, wearing a new bridle of polished leather with brass buckles and studs, and two white flowers in his ears. His mane was divided and curled, and each curl was tied with bows of colored ribbon. He had a girth of gold and silver around his body, and his tail was pleated with red and blue velvet ribbons. He was, in short, a lovely little donkey!

The ringmaster, in presenting him to the crowd, added these words: "My respectable audience! I am not here to tell you tall tales about the great difficulties that I had in capturing and subduing this mammal, while he was grazing, wild and free, among the mountains in the plains of the torrid zone. Observe the wild rolling of his eyes. Having tried, in vain, every gentle means to tame him and to accustom him to the life of domestic animals, I was often forced to correct him with the whip. But all my goodness to him, instead of gaining his affections, has, on the contrary, increased his viciousness. However, following the system of Gall, I discovered in his cranium a bony cartilage, which the Faculty of Medicine in Paris has recognized as the generator of hair—and of dance. Therefore, I have taught him not only to dance, but also to jump through hoops and frames covered with paper. Admire him, and then pass your judgment on him! But before taking my leave of you, permit me, ladies and gentlemen, to invite you to the daily performance that will take place tomorrow evening. In the

unfortunate event that the weather should threaten rain, the performance will be moved to tomorrow morning at eleven o'clock."

Here the ringmaster made another deep bow, and then, turning to Pinocchio, said, "Courage, Pinocchio! Before you begin your performance, bow to this distinguished audience—ladies, gentlemen, and children."

Pinocchio obeyed and bent both knees 'til they touched the ground. He remained kneeling until the ringmaster, cracking his whip, shouted, "Walk!"

Then the little donkey got up and began walking around the ring, keeping perfect step.

After a short while, the ringmaster cried, "Trot!" And Pinocchio, obeying the order, changed to a trot.

"Gallop!"

And Pinocchio broke into a gallop.

"Full gallop!"

And Pinocchio ran as fast as he could. Suddenly, while the little donkey was going full speed, the ringmaster, raising his arm in the air, fired a pistol.

At the shot, Pinocchio, pretending to be wounded, fell to the ground as if he were really dying.

As he got up from the ground, amidst an outburst of applause, shouts, and clapping of hands, he raised his head and looked up—and he saw in one of the boxes a beautiful lady who wore around her neck a thick gold chain, from which hung a medallion. On the medallion was the portrait of a puppet.

"That's my portrait! That lady is the fairy!" said Pinocchio to himself, recognizing her immediately. Overcome with delight, he tried to cry, "Oh, my little fairy! Oh, my dear fairy!"

But instead of these words, a bray came from his throat, so loud and prolonged that all the spectators laughed, especially the children.

The ringmaster, to teach him a lesson, and to make him understand that it is not good manners to bray before the public, gave Pinocchio a blow on his nose with the

handle of his whip.

The poor little donkey stuck his tongue out and licked his nose for at least five minutes to ease the pain.

But imagine his despair when, looking up a second time, he saw that the box was empty! The fairy had disappeared!

He thought he was going to die. His eyes filled with tears, and he began to weep. But nobody noticed, least of all the ringmaster, who, cracking his whip, shouted, "Courage, Pinocchio! Now let the audience see how gracefully you can jump through the hoops."

Pinocchio tried two or three times, but each time he came to the hoop, instead of going through it, he found it easier to go under it. At last he made a leap and went through, but his right leg caught in the hoop, causing him to fall to the ground, doubled up in a heap on the other side.

When he got up he was lame, and it was only with great difficulty that he managed to return to the stable.

"Bring out Pinocchio! We want the little donkey! Bring out the little donkey!" shouted all the children in the theater, disappointed by the sad accident.

But the little donkey was seen no more that evening.

The following morning the veterinarian—that is, a doctor of animals—paid him a visit and declared that he would remain lame for life.

The director of the company then said to the stable boy, "What do you suppose I can do with a lame donkey? He would eat food without earning it. Take him to the market and sell him."

When they reached the market, a buyer was found at once. He asked the stable boy, "How much do you want for that lame donkey?"

"Five dollars."

"I'll give you five cents. Don't think that I'm buying him to use. I'm buying him only for his skin. I see that his skin is very hard, and I intend to make a drum with it for the village band."

I leave it to my readers to imagine how poor Pinocchio felt when he heard that he was to become a drum!

As soon as the buyer had paid his five cents, he led the little donkey to the seashore. He put a stone around his neck and tied a long rope—the end of which he held in his hand—around his leg. He then gave him a sudden push, and Pinocchio was thrown into the water.

Pinocchio, weighed down by the stone, went immediately to the bottom. His owner, keeping a tight hold on the rope, sat down on a rock to wait until the little donkey had drowned, intending then to skin him.

⚜

{ Chapter 34 }

Pinocchio is swallowed by the terrible shark

fter Pinocchio had been underwater for almost an hour, his buyer said to himself, "My poor little lame donkey must be drowned by now. I'll pull him out of the water, and then make a fine drum of his skin."

He began to haul in the rope that he had tied to the donkey's leg. He hauled, and hauled, and hauled, until at last—what do you think appeared above the water? Instead of a dead donkey, the man saw a live puppet, wriggling like an eel!

When he saw the wooden puppet, the poor man thought he was dreaming. Struck dumb with astonishment, he stood with his mouth open, his eyes bulging out of his head.

Regaining some composure, he asked in a quavering voice, "And the little donkey that I threw into the sea? What's become of him?"

"I am the little donkey!" said Pinocchio, laughing.

"You?"

"I!"

"Ah, you young scamp, don't play any tricks on me!"

"Play tricks on you? My dear master, I'm speaking the truth."

"But how can you, who were a little donkey but a short time ago, have become a wooden puppet?"

"It must have been the effects of seawater. The sea can do extraordinary things."

"Be careful, puppet! Don't think that you can amuse yourself at my expense. Woe to you, if I lose patience!"

"Well, master, do you want to know the true story? If you free my leg from this rope, I'll tell it to you."

The man, who was curious to hear the true story, immediately untied the knot. Pinocchio, finding himself as free as a bird, began to speak as follows:

"You must know that I was once a puppet as I am now, and I was on the point of becoming a real boy, like so many others. But instead, because I didn't like to study, and because I listened to the advice of bad companions, I ran away from home. And one day when I awoke, I found myself changed into a donkey with long ears—and a long tail! What a disgrace it was to me—a disgrace, dear master, that the blessed St. Anthony would not inflict even upon you! I was taken to the market and sold to the director of a circus company, who decided to make a famous dancer of me, and a famous leaper through hoops. But one night, during a performance, I had a bad fall in the ring and lamed my leg. Then the director, not knowing what to do with a lame donkey, sent me to be sold, and you bought me!"

"That is only too true! I paid five cents for you. Now who will give me back my poor pennies?"

"And why did you buy me? You bought me to make a drum of my skin! A drum!"

"That's true! And now where will I find another skin?"

"Don't despair, master. There are so many little donkeys in the world!"

"Tell me, you impertinent rascal, does your story end here?"

"No," answered the puppet. "I have a few more words to say, and then I'll have finished. After you bought me, you brought me to this place to kill me. But then, yielding to a feeling of compassion, you preferred to tie a stone around my neck and throw me into the sea. This humane sentiment does you honor, and I'll always be grateful to you for it. Nevertheless, dear master, you made your plans without considering the fairy!"

"Who is this fairy?"

"She is my mother, and is like all other good mothers who care for their children and never lose sight of them, but help them lovingly, even when, because of their own foolishness and evil conduct, they deserve to be abandoned. Well, the good fairy, as soon as she saw that I was in danger of drowning, immediately sent an immense shoal of fish, who, believing me really to be a little dead donkey, began to eat me. And what mouthfuls they took! I would never have thought that fish were greedier than boys! Some ate my ears, some my muzzle, others my neck and mane, some the skin of my legs, and some my coat. Among them was a little fish so polite that he even condescended to eat my tail."

"From this day forward," said the horrified buyer, "I swear that I'll never eat fish again. It would be too dreadful to open a mullet, or a fried whiting, and find inside a donkey's tail!"

"I agree with you," said the puppet, laughing. "I must tell you that when the fish had finished eating the donkey's hide that covered me from head to foot, they naturally reached the bone, or rather, the wood. For as you see, I am made of the hardest wood. But after taking a few bites, they soon discovered that I was not a morsel for their teeth. Disgusted with such indigestible food, some went off in one direction, and some in another, without so much as a 'thank you.' And now at last I've told you how it came to be that when you pulled up the rope you found a live puppet instead of a dead donkey."

"Enough of your story!" cried the man in a rage. "I spent five cents to buy you, and I want my money back! Do you know what I'll do? I'll take you back to the market and sell you for firewood!"

"Sell me if you like. It makes no difference to me," said Pinocchio.

But as he said this, he leaped back into the water and, swimming happily away from the shore, called to his poor owner, "Good-bye, master! The next time you want a skin to make a drum, remember me!" And he laughed and went on swimming.

After a while he turned again and shouted louder, "Good-bye, master! The next time you want a little well-seasoned firewood, remember me!"

In the twinkling of an eye he had swum so far that he was barely visible. All that could be seen of him was a little black speck on the surface of the sea that from time to time lifted its legs out of the water and leaped and tumbled like a joyful dolphin.

Pinocchio was swimming, relaxed and carefree, when he saw a rock in the middle of the sea that seemed to be made of white marble. On top there stood a beautiful little goat, who bleated lovingly and gestured for him to come closer.

But the most peculiar thing was this: the little goat's hair, instead of being white or black, or a mixture of two colors, as is usual with other goats, was blue, and a very vivid blue, greatly resembling the hair of the beautiful child.

Imagine how quickly poor Pinocchio's heart began to beat. He swam with redoubled strength and energy toward the white rock. He was already halfway there when he saw, rising up out of the water and rushing toward him, the horrible head of a sea-monster. Its open, cavernous mouth and three rows of enormous teeth would have been terrifying to look at even in a picture.

And do you know what this sea-monster was?

It was none other than the gigantic shark who has been mentioned more than once in this story, and who, for its horrible killings and insatiable appetite, was called the "Attila of fish and fishermen."

Pinocchio was terrified at the sight of the monster. He tried to avoid it, to change his direction, or to swim faster than the monster. But that huge, gaping mouth came toward him as quickly as an arrow.

"Hurry, Pinocchio, for pity's sake!" cried the beautiful little goat, bleating.

Pinocchio swam desperately, using every ounce of his strength.

"Quick, Pinocchio, the monster is close behind you!"

Pinocchio swam quicker than ever, flying like a bullet from a gun. He had nearly reached the rock, and the little goat had stretched out her forelegs to help him out of the water—

But it was too late! The monster caught him and, drawing in its breath, sucked in the poor puppet as it might have sucked a hen's egg. Then it swallowed with such violence that Pinocchio, as he fell into the shark's stomach, was knocked unconscious for a quarter of an hour.

When he came to, he had no idea where he was. It was dark all around him, and the darkness was so deep that it seemed to him that he had fallen head-first into a bottle of ink. He listened, but he could hear no noise except for the great gusts of wind that blew in his face from time to time. At first, he did not know where the wind came from, but at last he discovered that it came from the monster's lungs. For you must know that the shark suffered from asthma, and when it breathed, it was exactly as if a north wind was blowing.

Pinocchio tried to keep up his courage, but when he was certain that he was trapped in the shark's body, he began to cry and scream and call out, "Help! Help! Oh, poor me! Will nobody come to save me?"

"Who do you think could save you, you unhappy wretch?" said a voice in the dark that sounded like a guitar out of tune.

"Who's there?" asked Pinocchio, frozen with terror.

"It is I—a poor tuna fish who was swallowed by the shark at the same time you were. And what kind of fish are you?"

"I have nothing in common with fish. I'm a puppet."

"If you're not a fish, why did you let yourself be swallowed by the monster?"

"I didn't let myself be swallowed. The monster swallowed me! And now what are we to do here in the dark?"

"Resign ourselves and wait until the shark has digested us."

"But I don't want to be digested!" howled Pinocchio, beginning to cry again.

"Neither do I," added the tuna fish, "but I'm wise enough to think that when one is born a tuna fish, it's more dignified to die in the water than in oil."

"Nonsense!" cried Pinocchio.

"That's my opinion," replied the tuna fish, "and opinions ought to be respected."

"Nevertheless, I want to get away from here. I want to escape!"

"Escape then, if you can!"

"Is this shark who has swallowed us very big?" asked the puppet.

"Big? His body is a mile long, not counting his tail."

While they were holding this conversation in the dark, Pinocchio thought he saw a light a long way off.

"What's that little light I see in the distance?" he asked.

"It's most likely some companion in misfortune who, like us, is waiting to be digested."

"I will go and find him. Do you think it may be some old fish who could perhaps show us how to escape?"

"I hope so, dear puppet."

"Good-bye, tuna fish."

"Good-bye, puppet, and may good fortune smile upon you."

"Where will we meet again?"

"Who knows? It's better not to think of it."

{ Chapter 35 }

Father and son together again

 aving said good-bye to the tuna fish, Pinocchio began to grope his way through the dark body of the shark, taking one step at a time in the direction of the dim light he saw shining at a great distance.

The farther he advanced, the brighter the light became. He walked and walked, until at last he reached it. And when he reached it, what did he find? I'll give you a thousand guesses. He found a little table, and on it a lighted candle stuck into a green glass bottle. And seated at the table was a little old man. He was eating some fish, and they were so much alive that they sometimes even jumped out of his mouth while he was eating them.

Seeing the old man, Pinocchio was filled with such great and unexpected joy that he became almost delirious. He wanted to laugh, to cry, and to say a thousand things, but he could only stammer out a few confused and broken words. Finally he succeeded in uttering a cry of joy and, throwing his arms around the little old man's neck, began to shout, "Oh, my dear father! I've found you at last! I'll never leave you again— never, never, never!"

"Do my eyes tell me the truth?" said the little old man, rubbing his eyes. "Are you really my dear Pinocchio?"

"Yes, yes, I am Pinocchio, really Pinocchio! And you have forgiven me, have you not? Oh, my dear father, how good you are! To think that I . . . Oh! But if you only knew what misfortunes have been poured upon my head, and all that has befallen me! Only imagine, the day that you, dear Father, sold your coat to buy me a spelling book so that I might go to school, I went to see the puppet show, and the Showman wanted to throw me on his fire so that I might roast his mutton. And he was the same man who later gave me five gold pieces to take to you, but I met the fox and the cat, who took me to the Lobster Inn, where they ate like wolves. And I left by myself in the middle of the night and encountered assassins, who ran after me, and I ran away, and they followed, and I ran, and they still followed me, and I ran, until they hung me from a branch of a tree called the Big Oak. And the beautiful child with blue hair sent a little carriage to fetch me. And when the doctors saw me, they said, 'If he is not dead, it's proof that he is still alive.' And then I told a lie, and my nose began to grow until I could no longer get through the door of the room, so I went with the fox and the cat to bury the four gold pieces, for one I had spent at the inn, and the parrot began to laugh, and instead of two thousand gold pieces, I found none, for which reason the judge, when he heard that I had been robbed, had me thrown into prison. And then, when I left the prison, I saw a bunch of grapes in a field, and I was caught in a trap, and the peasant, who had every right, put a dog collar around my neck to make me guard the poultry yard, but later, acknowledging my innocence, he let me go, and the serpent with the smoking tail began to laugh and broke a blood vessel. And so I returned to the house of the beautiful child, who was dead, and the pigeon, seeing that I was crying, said, 'I have seen your father. He was building a little boat to go in search of you.' And I said to him, 'Oh! If only I had wings,' and he said to me, 'Do you want to go to your father?' and I said, 'Without doubt! But who will take me to him?' and he said, 'I'll take you,' and I said, 'How?' and he said, 'Get on my back.' And so we flew all night, and in the morning, all the fishermen who were looking out to sea said, 'There is a poor man in a boat who is on the verge of being drowned,' and I recognized you at once, even at that distance, for my heart told me, and I made signs to you to return to land."

"I recognized you, too," said Geppetto, "and I would gladly have returned to the shore, but how could I? The sea was furious, and a great wave upset my boat. Then this horrible shark saw me in the water, took hold of me with its tongue, and swallowed me as if I had been a tart."

"How long have you been shut up here?" asked Pinocchio.

"Since that day. It must be nearly two years ago. Two years, my dear Pinocchio, that have seemed like two centuries!"

"And how have you managed to live? Where did you get the candle? And the matches to light it? Who gave them to you?"

"Stop, and I'll tell you everything. During that same storm in which my boat was overturned, a merchant vessel was heavily damaged. The sailors were all saved, but the vessel sank to the bottom, and the shark, who had a huge appetite that day, even after he had swallowed me, swallowed the vessel, too."

"How?"

"He swallowed it in one mouthful, and the only thing he spat out was the mainmast, which stuck between his teeth like a fish bone. Fortunately for me, the vessel was laden with preserved meat in tins, biscuits, bottles of wine, dried raisins, cheese, coffee, sugar, candles, and boxes of wax matches. With these provisions I've been able to live for two years. But I have reached the end of my supply. There's nothing left, and this candle that you see burning is the last one."

"And after that?"

"After that, dear boy, we'll both remain in the dark."

"Then, dear Father," said Pinocchio, "there's no time to lose. We must find a way to escape."

"Escape? But how?"

"We might escape through the shark's mouth, throw ourselves into the sea, and swim away."

"That's all very well, but, dear Pinocchio, I don't know how to swim."

"No matter. I'm a good swimmer. You can get on my back, and I'll carry you safely to shore."

"It's no use, my boy," replied Geppetto, shaking his head with a melancholy smile. "Do you think that a puppet like you, barely three feet tall, could have the strength to swim with me on his back?"

"Try it and see!"

Without another word, Pinocchio took the candle in his hand and said to his father, "Follow me, and don't be afraid."

So they walked for some time and traversed the body and the stomach of the shark. But when they arrived at the monster's throat, they thought it better to stop, take a look around, and choose the best moment for escaping.

Now I must tell you that the shark, being very old, and suffering from asthma and a weak heart, had to sleep with its mouth open. Pinocchio, therefore, having approached the monster's throat, looked up and saw a large strip of starry sky and beautiful moonlight beyond the enormous gaping mouth.

"This is the moment of escape," he whispered to his father. "The shark is sleeping like a mouse, the sea is calm, and it's as light as day. Follow me, dear Father, and we'll soon be free!"

They climbed up the throat of the monster, and when they reached its immense mouth, they began to walk on tiptoe down its tongue.

Before taking the final leap, the puppet said to his father, "Get on my back and put your arms around my neck. I'll take care of the rest."

As soon as Geppetto was firmly settled on his son's back, Pinocchio, feeling sure of himself, threw himself into the water and began to swim. The sea was smooth as oil, the moon shone brilliantly, and the shark was sleeping so soundly that even cannon fire would not have woken it.

{ Chapter 36 }

At last Pinocchio becomes a real boy

While Pinocchio was swimming quickly toward the shore, he discovered that his father, who was on his back, with his legs in the water, was trembling as violently as if the poor man had a fever.

Was he trembling from cold or from fear? Perhaps a little of both. But Pinocchio, thinking that it was from fear, said, "Courage, Father! In a few minutes we'll be safely on shore."

"But where is the shore?" asked the little old man, becoming still more frightened, and squinting his eyes as tailors do when they want to thread a needle. "I've been looking in every direction, and I see nothing but the sky and the sea."

"I can see the shore quite well," said the puppet. "You must know that I'm like a cat. I see better by night than by day."

Poor Pinocchio was pretending to be in good spirits, but in fact he was beginning to worry. His strength was failing, he was gasping and panting for breath, and the shore was still far off.

He swam until he had no breath left. Then he turned to Geppetto and said, "Father, help me! I'm dying!"

Father and son were on the verge of drowning when they heard a voice like a guitar out of tune, saying, "Who is dying?"

"It is I, and my poor father!"

"I know that voice! You're Pinocchio!"

"Yes! And who are you?"

"I am the tuna fish, your prison companion in the body of the shark."

"How did you manage to escape?"

"I followed your example. You showed me the way, and I escaped after you."

"Tuna fish, you've arrived just in time! I beg you to help us, or we are lost."

"Willingly and with all my heart! Take hold of my tail, and leave the rest to me. You will reach the shore in four minutes."

Geppetto and Pinocchio, as I need not tell you, accepted the offer at once. But instead of grabbing hold of the fish's tail, they thought it would be more comfortable to ride on the tuna's back.

Once they reached the shore, Pinocchio sprang onto the sand first and then helped his father. He then turned to the tuna fish and said in a voice full of emotion, "My friend, you have saved my father's life. I can find no words with which to thank you properly. Allow me at least to give you a kiss as a sign of my eternal gratitude!"

The tuna fish raised his head out of the water, and Pinocchio, kneeling on the ground, kissed him tenderly between the eyes. At this spontaneous show of affection, the poor tuna, who was not accustomed to it, was extremely moved and, ashamed to let himself be seen crying like a child, dove under the water and disappeared.

Meanwhile, day had dawned. Pinocchio offered his arm to Geppetto, who barely had breath to stand, and said, "Lean on my arm, dear Father, and let's go. We'll walk very slowly, like the ants, and when we're tired, we can rest by the wayside."

"And where will we go?" asked Geppetto.

"In search of some house or cottage where they will give us a mouthful of bread to eat and a little straw to sleep on."

They had not gone a hundred yards when they saw by the roadside two villainous-looking individuals begging.

They were the cat and the fox, but they were barely recognizable. The cat had pretended to be blind for so long that she really had become blind. And the fox, old, mangy, and with one side paralyzed, had lost his tail. That sneaking thief, having fallen into the most squalid misery, found himself obliged to sell his beautiful tail one day to a traveling peddler, who bought it to drive away flies.

"Oh, Pinocchio!" cried the fox. "Give a little charity to two poor invalids!"

"Invalids!" repeated the cat.

"Go away, impostors!" answered the puppet. "You cheated me once, but you will never cheat me again."

"Believe me, Pinocchio, we are now truly poor and miserable!"

"Poor and miserable!" repeated the cat.

"If you're poor and miserable, you deserve it. Remember the proverb: 'Stolen money never bears fruit.' Good-bye, impostors!"

"Have pity on us!"

"On us!"

"Good-bye, impostors! Remember the proverb: 'He who steals his neighbor's cloak ends his life without a shirt!'"

Upon saying this, Pinocchio and Geppetto went their way in peace. When they had gone another hundred yards, they saw a little cottage made of bricks and tiles, with a roof of straw.

"Someone must live there," said Pinocchio. "Let's go and knock at the door."

They went and knocked.

"Who's there?" said a little voice from within.

"We are a poor father and son without bread and without a roof," answered the puppet.

"Turn the key, and the door will open," said the same little voice.

Pinocchio turned the key, and the door opened. They went in and looked here, there, and everywhere, but they could see no one.

"Hello! Where's the master of the house?" said Pinocchio, much surprised.

"Here I am, up here!"

The father and son looked up to the ceiling, and there on a beam they saw the talking cricket.

"Oh, my dear little cricket!" said Pinocchio, bowing politely to him.

"Ah! Now you call me your 'dear little cricket.' But do you remember the time when you threw a mallet at me, to drive me from your house?"

"You're right, cricket! Drive me away, too! Throw a mallet at me, but have pity on my poor father."

"I'll have pity on both of you, but I wanted to remind you of the cruel treatment I received from you, to teach you that in this world, when it is possible, we should show courtesy to everybody, if we want it to be extended to us in our hour of need."

"You're right, cricket, you're right, and I'll remember the lesson you have given me. But tell me, how did you manage to buy this beautiful hut?"

"This hut was given to me yesterday by a goat whose wool was a beautiful blue color."

"And where has the goat gone?" asked Pinocchio with great curiosity.

"I don't know."

"When will it come back?"

"It will never come back. It went away yesterday, bleating in great grief as if to say, 'Poor Pinocchio. I'll never see him again. By this time, the shark must surely have devoured him!'"

"Did it really say that? Then it was she! It was she! It was my dear little fairy," exclaimed Pinocchio, sobbing bitterly.

When he had cried for some time, he dried his eyes and prepared a comfortable bed of straw for Geppetto. Then he asked the cricket, "Tell me, little cricket, where

can I find a glass of milk for my poor father?"

"A gardener named Giangio keeps cows three fields away from here. Go to him, and you might get some milk."

Pinocchio ran all the way to Giangio's house. Once there, the gardener asked him, "How much milk do you want?"

"A glassful."

"A glass of milk costs a penny. Where is your money?"

"I don't have any," replied Pinocchio, quite saddened.

"That's too bad," answered the gardener. "If you have no money for me, I have no milk for you."

"Patience!" said Pinocchio, and he turned to go.

"Wait a minute," said Giangio. "Perhaps we can manage something. Can you work a pumping machine?"

"What's a pumping machine?"

"It's a machine that draws up water from the well to water the vegetables."

"I can try."

"If you draw a hundred buckets of water, I'll give you a glass of milk."

"It's a deal!"

Giangio then led Pinocchio to the garden and taught him to operate the pumping machine. Pinocchio immediately set to work, but before he had drawn up the hundred buckets of water, the perspiration was pouring from his head to his feet. Never before had he worked so hard.

"Up 'til now," said the gardener, "the labor of turning the pumping machine was performed by my little donkey. But the poor animal is dying."

"May I go and see him?" said Pinocchio.

"Of course."

When Pinocchio went into the stable, he saw a little donkey stretched on the straw, worn out from hunger and overwork. After looking at him carefully, he said to himself, much troubled, "I'm sure I know this little donkey! His face is not new to me." And bending over him, he asked in donkey language, "Who are you?"

At this question the little donkey opened his dying eyes and answered in the same language, "I . . . am . . . Lamp . . . wick."

Then, closing his eyes again, he died.

"Oh, poor Lampwick!" said Pinocchio in a low voice. And taking a handful of straw, he dried a tear that was rolling down his face.

"Why do you grieve for a donkey that cost you nothing?" said the gardener. "I paid good money for him! Now what will I do?"

"I must tell you, he was my friend!"

"Your friend?"

"One of my schoolmates!"

"What?" shouted Giangio, laughing loudly. "You had donkeys for schoolmates? I can only imagine what wonderful lessons you must have had!"

The puppet, who felt very ashamed by these words, did not answer, but took his glass of milk and returned to the hut.

From that day forward, for more than five months, he continued to get up at daybreak every morning to go and work the pumping machine, to earn a glass of milk for his father. But that wasn't all he did. During his spare time, he learned to make woven baskets, and with the money he made by selling them, he was able to pay for all their needs. He also constructed an elegant little wheelchair, in which he could take his father out for fresh air when the weather was fine.

He not only succeeded in taking care of his poor father, but he also managed to put aside forty cents to buy himself a new coat.

One morning he said to his father, "I'm going to the market to buy a jacket, a cap, and a pair of shoes. When I return," he added, laughing, "I'll be so well dressed that you'll mistake me for a fine gentleman."

After leaving the house, he began to run merrily and happily along. Suddenly, he heard someone call his name. He turned around and saw a big snail crawling out from the hedge.

"Don't you know me?" asked the snail.

"Perhaps—and yet I'm not sure."

"Don't you remember the snail who served the fairy with blue hair? Don't you remember the time when I came downstairs to let you in, and you were caught by your foot, which you had stuck through the front door?"

"I remember it all," shouted Pinocchio. "Tell me quickly, my beautiful little snail, where have you left my good fairy? What is she doing? Has she forgiven me? Does she still remember me? Does she still love me? Is she far from here? Can I go and see her?"

The snail replied with her usual slowness, "My dear Pinocchio, the poor fairy is lying in bed at the hospital!"

"At the hospital?"

"It's only too true. Overtaken by a thousand misfortunes, she has fallen very ill, and she doesn't even have enough money to buy herself a mouthful of bread."

"Is it really so? Oh, what sorry news you have given me! Oh, poor fairy! Poor, poor fairy! If I had a million dollars, I would carry it to her immediately! But I have only forty pennies. With them I was going to buy a new coat. But take them, snail, and carry them at once to my good fairy."

"And your new coat?"

"What does a new coat matter? I would even sell these rags I have on if it would help her. Go, snail, and be quick; and in two days return to this place, for I hope I'll then be able to give you some more money. Up until now I've worked to take care of my father. From now on, I'll work five hours more each day so that I may also take care of my good mother. Good-bye, snail! I'll expect you in two days!"

The snail, most surprisingly, began to run like a lizard under the hot August sun.

That evening, instead of going to bed at ten o'clock, Pinocchio sat up 'til midnight, and instead of making eight woven baskets, he made sixteen.

Then he went to bed and fell asleep. And while he slept, he thought he saw the fairy, smiling and beautiful, who kissed him and said, "Well done, Pinocchio! To reward you for your good heart, I'll forgive you for all your past misdeeds. Boys who take care of their parents, and help them when they are poor and sick, are deserving of great praise and affection, even if they are not models of obedience and good behavior. Try and do better in the future, and you'll be happy."

Then the dream ended, and Pinocchio opened his eyes and awoke.

Imagine his astonishment when he discovered that he was no longer a wooden puppet, but a boy, a boy like all other boys! He looked around and saw that the straw roof of the hut had disappeared. He was in a pretty little room that was simply but elegantly furnished and arranged. Jumping out of bed, he found a new suit of clothes ready for him, a new cap, and a pair of new leather boots that fit him beautifully.

When he was dressed, he put his hands in his pockets—and pulled out a little ivory purse on which these words were written: "The fairy with blue hair returns the forty cents to her dear Pinocchio, and thanks him for his good heart." He opened the purse, and instead of forty copper pennies, he found forty shining gold pieces.

He then went and looked at himself in the mirror, and he thought he was someone else. For he no longer saw the usual reflection of a wooden puppet. He was greeted instead by the reflection of a bright, intelligent boy with chestnut hair and blue eyes, looking contented and full of joy.

In the midst of all these wonders, Pinocchio felt quite bewildered, and he could not tell if he was really awake or dreaming with his eyes open.

"Where can my father be?" he exclaimed suddenly, and going into the next room, he found old Geppetto quite well, lively, and in good spirits, just as he had been long ago. He had already resumed his wood-carving, and he was designing a rich and beautiful frame of leaves, flowers, and animal heads.

"Tell me, dear Father," said Pinocchio, throwing his arms around his neck and covering him with kisses. "How can this sudden change be explained?"

"This sudden change is all your doing," answered Geppetto.

"How is it my doing?"

"Because when children who have been naughty turn over a new leaf and become good, they have the power to bring happiness to their families."

"And the old wooden Pinocchio, where is he?"

"There he is," answered Geppetto, and he pointed to a big puppet leaning against a chair, its head on one side, its arms dangling, and its legs so crossed and bent that it was really a miracle that it remained standing.

Pinocchio turned and looked at it for a moment, and then said happily to himself, "How ridiculous I was when I was a puppet! And how glad I am to be a real boy at last!"

The End

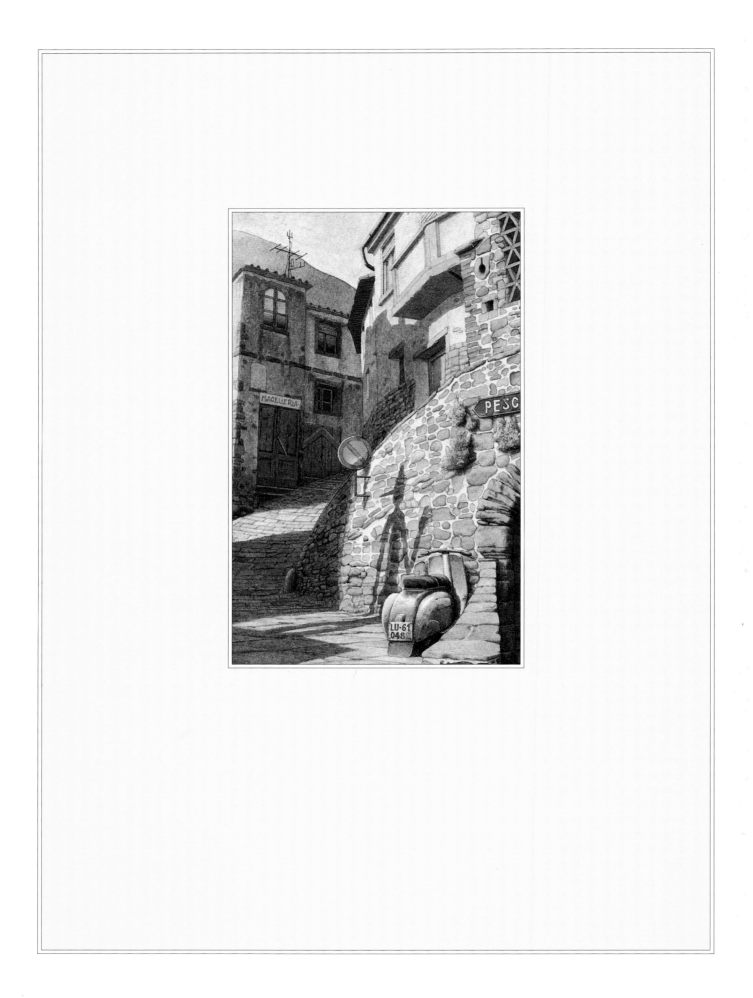